# AMULETS OF ACACIA

# AMULETS OF ACACIA

*William Meehan*

iUniverse, Inc.

New York  Lincoln  Shanghai

# Amulets of Acacia

iUniverse, Inc.

For information address:
iUniverse, Inc.
2021 Pine Lake Road, Suite 100
Lincoln, NE 68512
www.iuniverse.com

ISBN: 0-595-27163-4 (pbk)
ISBN: 0-595-74755-8 (cloth)

Printed in the United States of America

For all of their love and support,
This book is dedicated to my family:
Bill, Marjorie, Diane, and Scott;
And to God,
Who has blessed us all with so much.

*Special thanks to Chas Hoar, Greg Downing, John Hoar, Mary and Ali Earon, David Replogle, Ron Amack, Diane Norby, Mona Henry, and to all of my wonderful students who read initial drafts with enthusiastic honesty. Their comments and reactions went far in shaping the final product.*

# Contents

Prologue . . . . . . . . . . . . . . . . . . . . . . . . . . . . . . . . . . . . . . 1

Chapter 1    On to Grandpa's . . . . . . . . . . . . . . . . . . . . 5

Chapter 2    The Weeping Desk . . . . . . . . . . . . . . . 13

Chapter 3    Amulets of Acacia . . . . . . . . . . . . . . . . 20

Chapter 4    Into the Orb . . . . . . . . . . . . . . . . . . . . . 27

Chapter 5    The Girl by the Bank . . . . . . . . . . . . . . . 31

Chapter 6    Return to Acacia . . . . . . . . . . . . . . . . . . 39

Chapter 7    Lewis & Chas . . . . . . . . . . . . . . . . . . . . . 50

Chapter 8    Dryden . . . . . . . . . . . . . . . . . . . . . . . . . 66

Chapter 9    On to the Castle . . . . . . . . . . . . . . . . . . 77

Chapter 10   Attack of the Beasts . . . . . . . . . . . . . . 90

Chapter 11   Roland Reports . . . . . . . . . . . . . . . . 101

Chapter 12   Showdown! . . . . . . . . . . . . . . . . . . . . 114

Chapter 13   Wherein All That's Good Returns . . . . . . . . 126

Chapter 14   Back at Grandpa's . . . . . . . . . . . . . . . 139

Author's Note . . . . . . . . . . . . . . . . . . . . . . . . . . . . . . 145

Alternate Beginning . . . . . . . . . . . . . . . . . . . . . . . . . 147

# *Prologue*

"Where are yeh now?" the old man mumbled to himself as he leaned on a nearby table to catch his breath. "C'mon now. I know you're in here somewhere. I can feel yeh."

The old man was tired, and his back ached from being on his feet all morning, but he refused to let it slow him down—not now. Everything would be cleared out by Sunday's end, auctioned off to the highest bidders. This would be his last chance to get *them* back; he was sure of it. He had to get them back. He couldn't risk letting it happen again—ever.

The old man caught his breath and continued rummaging down rows of mismatched furniture and sifting through tables of scattered belongings. Normally, nothing would bring him more joy than to shuffle through the items at a simple neighborhood yard sale or at an old antique shop. He still managed to find wonder in things long since considered wonderful—but not today.

The old man slumped heavily onto a wooden chair and sank his head into his hands. "Please, Good Spirits, I need your help," he whispered. "Just give me a sign…any—"

The old man's head rose slowly. It was a voice—a voice that was different from those murmuring about the room. It was soft, yet troubled—a young girl's; he was certain—but it had a different echo to it as if it had sounded from a distant place that was not of the room. She spoke words the old man couldn't understand...no, not words...she was weeping.

The old man quickly scanned the room. No one else browsing about the items seemed to take notice. He fought hard to control the tears of relief that welled in his eyes. "Thank you," he sighed in exhaustion, his voice barely that of a whisper. Things had gotten worse—far worse—he was sure of it, and the fault was his.

The sobbing led the old man to a worn, wooden desk on the backside of the room and abruptly stopped as he reached it. *It can't be*, he told himself. He was sure he had already checked the old desk before.

The old man stepped back and sized it up once again. There was nothing really appealing about the desk, three drawers down the left-hand side and one across the middle. And to make matters worse, nothing but an over-sized nail held the front, right leg on—hardly worth bidding on. It was more likely to see the dump than the auction block.

The old man opened each desk drawer again, but, as expected, they were empty. "C'mon, you must be here somewhere," he murmured as he reached under and slid a hand across the desk's underside.

"Can I be of assistance, sir?"

A tall, lanky man with a long, thin head was leaning over the old man's shoulder. A pair of thick, black glasses sat on the tip of the man's nose, magnifying his eyes to double their normal size. It gave him the appearance of a bug of sorts—*a grasshopper*, thought the old man.

The old man hesitated. "Ah...just interested in the desk...for my grandsons."

"I see," replied the tall, thin man. "A bit of a fixer-upper. Are you handy?"

"I do enjoy tinkering," answered the old man.

"Well, I'm sure we could get this item up quickly for you. Just give a holler if you decide that you want it."

The old man watched as the tall, thin man ambled over to a young couple that was examining a dining room table. The old man let out a deep breath; he would have to be careful.

He turned back to the desk and examined it more closely: back to front, top to bottom—nothing. *There has to be a hidden drawer here somewhere*, but where?

He opened the drawers once again and inspected them carefully. A slow smile spread across the old man's face. "How clever," he said aloud, shaking his head. He reached into the lowest drawer and rapped on its bottom. Just as he had expected—*hollow*. The drawer wasn't as deep on the inside as its outward length indicated. Sliding a hand across the bottom of the drawer, the old man pushed down on the rear of the drawer's casing. As he pushed down on the back end, the front end popped up revealing the hidden compartment beneath.

"I'll take it!" hollered the old man to the tall, thin man, who was quite taken aback by the old man's abruptness; so much so, that his wide-eyed look most definitely reminded the old man of a grasshopper.

# CHAPTER 1

# On to Grandpa's

"Entering Massachusetts!" blurted Scott.

Mother just smiled. Scott didn't get quite as excited as he used to when the faded-blue sign came into view, but he still yelled it out anyway. He had taken over the role several years before by beating Mother to the punch one trip and had assumed the duty ever since. It was a matter of tradition now.

On one trip when Scott was about six, Mother had actually pulled the car over so she and Scott could jump back and forth across the state line. Scott had told everyone that summer how he had jumped from Rhode Island to Massachusetts. It was one of his favorite memories. He still remembered it with a smile every time they passed the old sign.

"We'll be there before you know it," said Mother, watching Scott in the rearview mirror.

Scott just leaned his head back against the window. They had been driving now for almost four hours, and he was fresh out of ways to entertain himself. The bag of chips had been emptied a good hour before, and his eyes were too tired to read any more from the book he was reading about the Civil

War called *Fife*. He had had enough reading for one day, anyway.

Will, his older brother, was sprawled out in the front seat with his headphones on and was staring straight ahead with a blank expression. This was the first year that Will had given Mother a hard time about going to Grandpa's—something about missing out on everything. He had barely spoken a word since they left, and his headphones were blaring so loudly that Scott could make out the songs from the back seat.

They had been making this ride at the beginning of every summer for as long as Scott could remember. Mother felt it was important for the boys to spend time with their grandfather, so just after school closing each year, they would pack their bags and head north to spend a week at Grandpa's. For Scott and Will it came to mark the beginning of summer vacation.

Gramps lived in a small ranch-style house near a lake that was surrounded by towering pines. Will once heard Gramps say that he owned more than fourteen acres of land, and it was chock-full of places to explore and things to do. Their old tree fort would be in need of repair, and Ol' Bess was still out there for the taking, a two-foot bass that was as sly as an old fox. Scott came close to pulling her in last year, but Bess snapped the line before Gramps could get a net on her—maybe this year.

The trip was special for Mother too. For her it meant relaxation. She would say the trip was spiritual—a week to take it easy and leave all the pressures of life behind. She and Gramps would search out yard sales and take long walks through the woods and talk about nothing and everything. Gramps pampered her the entire stay, and Mother gladly let him. Gramps knew how hard she worked to take care of the boys and felt it was the least she deserved.

Mother was a gentle woman and the glue that held the family together, especially after Scott and Will's father had passed away several years before. It was a difficult time for all of them, but she somehow found the strength to pull them all through it. Their trips to Grandpa's took on even more importance then.

Scott was a surprisingly tall, but reedy, ten-year-old with straight brown hair and deep blue eyes. Though an average student, he had a kind heart and was well liked at school. He was a good athlete too. Hockey and baseball were his favorites, and he was good at both.

Will had just turned fifteen and was experimenting with growing his hair long. He had curly hair, and Scott thought it was just getting puffier, but Will thought it made him look older. He had been taking guitar lessons for the past year and had just started a band with some of the guys at school.

Will was at the age where it wasn't cool to be hanging out with family, so he decided to just tune them out instead. Mother refused to let it dampen her spirits though. She was too excited about seeing her father to let it.

"Just ten more minutes," she announced, noticing Scott's boredom (That seemed to be one of her favorite lines.).

"That's what you said ten minutes ago," moaned Scott.

"We're almost there. The old clock tower's right up ahead."

The first sight of the old clock tower always welled up a special feeling inside of Scott's chest. The tower was atop an old church and had read 6:33 for the past fourteen years. It was a well-known landmark in the area. Even Will took off his headphones at the sight of it.

"I think I can smell Grandpa's chili already," chuckled Mother.

Every summer it was the same thing. They would pull up, and Gramps would bounce down the porch stairs yelling, "Hurry up! The chili's ready, and it's burning a hole through the pot!"

It was good chili, but the taste lingered for days. Gramps loved it hot. In fact, he loved everything hot. He even put Tabasco sauce on his eggs in the morning much to the boys' disgust.

"Are you going to try to catch Ol' Bess this year?" Mother asked Will in an attempt to arouse some excitement in him.

It looked as if Will was starting to come around. The sight of the old clock tower couldn't help but stir up good memories, but he stubbornly continued to brood. "Maybe," he muttered.

"Hey, Will, do you think the fort's still up?" asked Scott, tugging at Will's shoulder.

Will tried to shrug him off but finally caved in and smiled for the first time since they left. Though Will would never admit it, he was curious himself to see how the old fort had survived. "We can check it out tomorrow if you want," he offered and reached back to tousle Scott's hair.

As they made the sharp right at *Mama Pedroli's Pizza & Pastrami,* they started down the long dirt road that would lead them to their grandfather's. A kind of hushed excitement came over them as it did every year when they turned down the old dirt way.

The road was always dry, and, as usual, the dust engulfed the car, temporarily blinding them, but as the car slowed, the dust began to settle, and Grandpa's house slowly came into view.

The old place never seemed to change, thought Scott. The faded shingles may have been a bit more faded, but the same dented red mailbox hung unevenly by the door, the same assortment of worn wicker chairs littered the porch, and the same gray statue of a lion sat stoically at the bottom stair (Gramps had spotted it at some old yard sale.). "He guards the property," Gramps would say of the stone beast.

As the car sputtered to a halt, Mother gave a couple of *toots* on the horn. As if on cue, Gramps came bounding out the front door. "Hurry up!" he puffed.

"We know," smiled Will, as he opened the car door. "The chili's ready, and it's burning a hole in the pot."

"Dang tootin'!" cried Gramps. "Leave them bags in the car. We'll get 'em later. Now get over here and give me a hug before my house burns down!"

Gramps was a surprisingly robust man for his age. He had arms like a bear and gave the kind of hugs that swallowed you whole. Though they always kept in touch throughout the year, it felt good to see him again.

A large stone fireplace dominated the inside of the house, and the kitchen featured the longest oak table the boys had ever seen. Gramps loved to go hunting for antiques, and there wasn't a yard sale for miles around that he didn't sniff out. He furnished his house this way. It was full of odd furnishings and knick-knacks, mostly old and what might seem like junk to others, but a *find* for Gramps. All that stuff, though, seemed to find its proper place and provided the house with a warm, homey feeling.

Four bowls of piping-hot chili were already sitting on the kitchen table when they stepped in. They sat right away, and Gramps took a loaf of warm bread out of the oven. The sweet aroma filled the room reminding them all of how hungry they were. Gramps sliced them each a large piece and smothered them with butter. They plunged into the chili. Though it always took a couple of bites and a few gulps of water before they got used to the spice, they were hungry, and that made it seem even more delicious.

"Boy, you two have gotten big!" exclaimed Gramps. "Your mom must be feedin' you pretty good back home."

"They eat me out of house and home!" giggled Mother.

"Did I tell you, boys, I almost caught Ol' Bess?" said Gramps. "I had her on the line for almost half a minute before she broke free. I'm countin' on you two to finally bring her in this year."

"We'll have her in the pan by week's end," promised Will.

Gramps snorted in approval and rumpled Will's hair. "Now finish up that chili, everyone!" he bellowed. "I've got an apple pie warming in the oven and a full pint of cookie-dough ice cream in the freezer."

"Awesome!" cried Scott.

"How about you, Mums?" Gramps asked. "Pie and ice cream?"

"Only if you promise to walk it off with me tomorrow," she replied.

"Deal," Gramps agreed.

After dinner the boys got their bags from the car and dragged them into the room that they would share for the next week. The room hadn't changed much over the years. It consisted of a large wooden bunk bed and matching bureaus. A painting of a mare and her foal hung over one of the bureaus, and an old floor lamp stood next to the other (Gramps had surely found them at some old yard sale.). In the far corner of the room by the bureaus was a door that led to an adjacent bathroom and directly across from that, a closet. The trains that dotted the wallpaper seemed cool when they were younger but were a bit embarrassing now.

The only new addition to the room was an old desk sitting under the window on the far wall.

"Look at that thing," Will snickered. "It's got a nail holding the leg on."

Scott shook his head. "I hope Gramps doesn't think we'll be doing any studying while we're here."

"Maybe it's your birthday present," teased Will.

"Real funny, mushroom head," cracked Scott.

"You're just jealous," scoffed Will, as he mockingly ran his fingers through his puffy hair. "Go see if anything's in it."

Scott tossed his bag on the floor and reached for the desk's bottom drawer. Just as he took hold of the handle, Mother poked her head into the room. Both boys jumped. "I'm sorry. I didn't mean to startle you," she chuckled. "Your grandfather is starting a fire. We can play some cards before you head to bed if you want."

"Sounds good," said Will, forgetting about the desk. "Tell Gramps he's goin' down this year."

*Rummy 500* was the game, and Gramps was the champ. He would always hold on to all of his *straights* and *threes-of-a-kind* and wait for that one card he needed to go out and leave everyone stranded with all of their cards. Will came close to beating him once last year, but Gramps stuck him with two *aces* in the final hand to win the game.

"C'mon," said Will. "We can finish unpacking tomorrow. You're going down, too."

Scott just rolled his eyes. He always got creamed when they played cards, and he really wasn't in the mood for another humiliating defeat. Will rushed out to the den leaving Scott with little choice. Before following, Scott paused before the old desk and again reached for the bottom drawer. A weird feeling suddenly struck him causing him to pull back. At first he thought it might have been the chili, but he couldn't seem to shake it. It wasn't a bad feeling, but he wouldn't say it was a good feeling, either. It was just a feeling that something was about to happen—*something big.*

# CHAPTER 2

# *The Weeping Desk*

Scott hadn't realized how tired he was until he settled down at the table to play cards. The drive had really knocked him out, and he found himself dozing off as the game wore on. He was losing, anyway. Gramps was way ahead as usual and kept whistling some annoying tune from about fifty years ago. Will was really irritated.

Mother was hanging in there, but it didn't really matter to her whether she won or lost; it never did. She just loved the fact that everyone was together. "Why don't you head to bed," she whispered to Scott. "You'll need your rest if you're going to rebuild the fort tomorrow."

Scott nodded wearily and forced himself up with a yawn. "You win, Gramps," he conceded.

Gramps sprung from his chair and rumpled Scott's hair (He was always doing that.). "You played me hard this year, *Tiger.* C'mon. I'll walk you down to the room."

"Make sure you come back," Will barked at Gramps. "This ain't over yet."

Will never did take losing very well. Gramps was up by over a hundred points and was holding on to his cards again. That meant trouble for Will.

Scott smirked as he entered the bedroom. "Looks like I get the top bunk."

Gramps stooped to click on a chipped metal fan that was resting on the near bureau. "First come—first served. You sleep tight now, you hear?"

"Thanks, Gramps," smiled Scott. It certainly did feel good to be with Gramps again.

Gramps leaned over and kissed Scott on the forehead. "Now to finish off that grumpy, ol' brother of yours," he snorted and with a quick wink gently closed the door behind him.

Scott threw on a T-shirt and the worn flannel shorts he usually wore to bed and went into the bathroom to wash-up. When he finished, he climbed onto the top bunk, clicked off the light, and settled under the covers. He enjoyed the minutes lying in bed before sleep overtook him; it was when he did his best thinking. Tonight, though, he was exhausted and fading quickly.

As Scott's thoughts swirled into dream, a strange noise jolted him awake. It sounded like crying. He strained to listen further, but the room had settled back into silence. Probably just Will losing, he figured, and with a quick yawn, rolled back onto his side.

As his thoughts drifted away once more, the strange sound again filled the room. Somebody was definitely crying, and it wasn't Will. It was a young girl, and it was coming from the closet.

In one frantic move Scott leaned over the side of the bunk and flipped on the light. Tumbling out from the bunk, he lunged towards the door and reached for the knob but paused as another soft whimper echoed from behind. Every instinct was telling him to get out, but instead, Scott found himself moving towards the closet door as if a huge human magnet of sorts were pulling him toward it.

Scott paused before the closet and slowly reached for the handle. It felt cold on his skin. His hand shook. With a deep breath he pushed down on the handle and pulled open the door. He was set to make a run for it, but when he peeked in, there was nothing there but an assortment of old clothes.

Gramps should definitely check this out, he decided, and retreated toward the bedroom door. But just as he reached it again, he was halted once more by the weeping that continued on from behind him. He had been wrong. It wasn't coming from the closet. It seemed to be coming from under the old desk that stood next to it. Could a small girl be crouched underneath it? Scott leaned to peek under the desk, but there was nobody there that he could see. Oddly, though, the sobbing continued.

Inching closer, Scott paused before the desk and examined it more closely. The crying wasn't coming from beneath it, he realized, but seemed to be coming from inside it—the bottom drawer. But that's impossible, he thought. The drawer was less than a foot high. A mouse or something must have gotten itself trapped in the drawer, but didn't it sound for all the world like a young girl.

Scott reached for the drawer's handle and pulled the drawer slightly open. The sobs coming from the drawer abruptly stopped. He pulled the drawer open another inch or so and peered in but couldn't make anything out within the drawer. He was sure that whatever it was, was cowering against the back, but when he opened the drawer a few inches more, there was still nothing to be seen. Scott let out a surprised snort and pulled the drawer completely open. It was empty!

Scott stared dumbfounded at the desk. He slowly opened the rest of the drawers, half expecting a baby animal or something to pop out at him, but they were all empty. Baffled, he checked beneath the desk again and behind it as well, but his search turned up empty.

As Scott peered into the bottom drawer one last time, Will strolled into the room. "Gramps won again," he moaned. Scott quickly closed all of the desk's drawers and moved away from the desk. "Enjoying your birthday present, I see," said Will.

Scott's face was chalk white. "Will, I know you're not going to believe me, but I heard noises coming from the desk. It sounded like a girl was crying, but there's nothing in it."

"Didn't Gramps tell you?" asked Will. "The desk is haunted. It used to belong to a girl who died a mysterious death while doing her homework. To this very day, they say her spirit's still trying to finish that homework. You'd be crying too if you'd been working on homework for fifty years and still hadn't finished."

"I'm serious, Will," said Scott.

Scott was visibly upset, and it only took one glance from Will to see that Scott wasn't fooling around. "Hey, are you okay?" Will asked.

"Please, Will. There's something wrong with the desk," Scott pleaded.

Will looked at the desk and back at Scott. He hesitated but walked over to the desk and knelt before it. "I don't hear anything."

"Just check it out," Scott urged.

Will cautiously raised a hand and opened the middle drawer a few inches. He carefully peered inside, but it was empty. He next checked the top-left drawer and then the second drawer, but they were empty as well. Scott held his breath as Will reached for the bottom drawer and slowly pulled it open. Will suddenly tumbled back. "What the heck?" he gasped as the sobs of a young girl echoed from the open drawer. "Is this a joke?"

Scott was scared, to be sure, but was glad that Will had also heard the crying. He had almost thought for a moment that he really might have been going crazy. "You hear it too?" Scott asked.

"Yeah," Will answered. He looked as if he were hearing a ghost. "Is that somebody crying?"

"It sounds like a girl," said Scott, "but there's nothing there that I can see."

Will quickly closed the bottom drawer. The crying stopped as soon as the drawer closed. "We should get Gramps. Maybe he knows something about it," said Will. "Call for Gramps…and try to act normal, if you can do that. Don't say anything about the crying either."

Scott poked his head out into the hall and called for Gramps.

"Is everything all right?" answered Mom, from down the hall.

"Yeah, fine, Mom," Scott replied. "We just need to ask Gramps something."

"I'm on my way, *Tiger*," puffed Gramps, as he lumbered down to the bedroom. "What's up, boys?" he asked, poking his head into the room.

"We were just wondering where you got that desk from, Gramps," said Will.

"It's a bit beaten up, I know, but I plan on fixing it up," said Gramps. "I got it at an auction a few towns over. It belonged to a man that had disappeared two years back or so," Gramps explained. "A strange case. It still baffles the police. The bank took over his house and auctioned it off along with all the furniture in it. I know it ain't much to look at, but every bedroom should have a desk in it."

As Gramps explained the story, he ambled over to the desk and reached for the bottom drawer. Scott and Will held their breath, but when Gramps opened the drawer, no sound escaped from it! Nothing! Why hadn't the drawer started crying when Gramps opened it? Gramps took a quick peek inside the drawer and closed it tightly. "Yep, every bedroom needs a desk. When yeh come back to visit again, I'll have her looking like new."

Scott looked at Will and shrugged his shoulders.

"Anything else I can help you boys with?" asked Gramps.

"No," answered Will, a bit dazed. "Thanks."

They didn't dare say anything about the crying drawer now that nothing happened when Gramps opened it. He'd think they were both crazy.

Gramps wished them a good night and left the boys staring dumbly at each other. Will walked over to the desk and opened the bottom drawer once again. To his surprise, it remained silent. "It's back to normal," he pointed out.

"What happened, Will?"

"I don't know, Scott. Maybe Grandpa's chili finally got to us."

Neither of them really believed this, but they left it at that for now. Scott climbed back onto the top bunk while Will washed up. Scott looked down at the old desk. He knew it really happened, and it wasn't Grandpa's chili either. Will came in from the bathroom, keeping a safe distance from the desk, and reached for the light switch.

"Will?"

"Yeah?" he answered.

"Do you mind if we keep the light on for a while?"

"No, that's okay," Will answered. He really didn't mind having the light on for a while himself.

"Do you think she'll come back, Will…the girl crying?"

"I don't know, Scott…I really don't know."

Both boys lay quietly in their beds for what seemed like hours, just staring at the odd desk before sleep finally overtook them both.

# CHAPTER 3

# *Amulets of Acacia*

Both boys found themselves that night in dreams that swirled around the desk. Will dreamed of water gushing out from the desk's drawers. The bedroom quickly filled with water. There was no escape. He thrashed and rolled in his bed as he desperately tried to reach air in his dream. Panic overwhelmed him until his dream suddenly transformed with the soft melody of a ballad that was so sweet and pure that he found himself floating peacefully upwards as the heavenly song guided him to the surface and fresh air. No longer was he in the bedroom but floating upon a pond in the middle of a lovely forest. He gazed up at a moon and endless stars as he floated about, feeling at total peace within his new environment.

Scott dreamed of a hand that shot out from the desk's drawer and grabbed him by the arm. The grip was strong. He couldn't pull away. It was pulling him towards the desk. His body jerked in bed as he struggled with the powerful hand of his dream. Suddenly, he too heard a song—a wonderful and beautiful song. It had an instant calming effect. The hand abruptly let go and disappeared back into the drawer as Scott slipped into a peaceful dream in which he found himself floating on water in a state of total tranquility.

The window's shade wasn't drawn completely allowing for the morning sunlight to pour in. Scott's eyes opened slowly, struggling with the fresh light as his surroundings came into focus, but was he still hearing the singing?

Scott shot up in bed and quickly scanned the room. The sweet song that floated through his dreams was still being sung, and it was coming from the desk.

Scott swung his head over the edge of the bunk and reached down to grab Will's shoulder. "Will, wake up!" he whispered. "Wake up!"

Will roused with a start. "What?" he grunted and then instantly realized that he, too, was still hearing the tender ballad that had come to his rescue in his dream. "I heard that song in my dream last night," he whispered.

"Me, too. It's coming from the desk."

The singing abruptly stopped. The boys stared anxiously at the desk waiting for the melody to continue, but only the sounds of a waking house filled the air.

Mother poked her head into the room. "Are you boys going to sleep all morning? I need your help out in the kitchen. I'm making pancakes, and your grandfather's trying to put hot sauce in the batter. Quick!"

Will put on a smile. "We'll be right out."

"Should we tell them?" whispered Scott.

Will hesitated. "It seems to keep stopping whenever they come in. They're never going to believe us, and Mom will just start worrying. Let's just wait and see if anything else happens."

The boys threw on their jeans and sneakers and started for the kitchen but before leaving, took a last, uneasy glance back at the desk.

"Get away from those pancakes, Gramps!" yelled Will, as he entered the kitchen. "My tongue is still trying to recover from your chili last night!"

"A little spice never hurt no pancakes," snickered Gramps.

"You're gross, Gramps!" snorted Scott.

Mother made good pancakes—big and fluffy—and Gramps made the syrup himself from a maple tree out back. It was sweet, thick, and delicious.

The batter was saved from Grandpa's hot sauce, but his pancakes weren't so lucky. He smothered each cake not only with syrup, but with Tabasco sauce as well.

"That's disgusting!" moaned Scott.

"Have you ever tried it?" asked Gramps.

Scott just stuck his tongue out in disgust.

Mother laughed. "Your grandfather and I are going hunting for yard sales today. Do you boys want to come?"

Will had the syrup bottle turned completely upside down and was drowning his pancakes in syrup. "Nah, I think I'm going to see if the old tree fort is still up," he replied.

"Me, too," added Scott.

"That sounds fun," Mother smiled. "Just make sure you boys stay together, okay?"

"We will," mumbled Will, through a mouthful of pancake. Will always ate like it was his last meal.

After breakfast Mother and Gramps got ready to leave for their day of rummaging while Scott and Will put on clean shirts and made plans to head out to the old fort.

Mom kissed them both before she left. "Now be careful," she warned.

"Watch out for mountain lions," teased Gramps.

"There's no mountain lions out there, Gramps!" exclaimed Will.

"There's bears," he said with a growl.

Mother gave Gramps a playful slap on the arm. "Stop that, Dad! You'll scare Scott."

"I'm not scared!" shot Scott. "I know there's no bears out there!"

"And make sure you stay clear of the snakes," hissed Gramps. "There's some nasty ones out there."

"That's enough," giggled Mother. "Let's go before the boys decide to stay in."

Gramps laughed and carefully placed his exploring hat on his head, the lucky exploring hat—nothing but a limp leather cowboy hat of sorts. Gramps never left the house without it and had owned it for as long as Scott and Will could remember. Mom used to try to talk him into getting a new hat, but Gramps refused to part with his lucky exploring hat.

As Mother closed the door behind them, the boys quickly set about gathering supplies for their day ahead. Scott headed for the basement to find a hammer and some nails while Will headed out back to sort through a pile of discarded wood behind the shed. Most of the wood had rotted out, but some of the boards underneath had been sheltered from the weather and were still in good shape. Will set aside a few of the sturdier boards and headed back into the house to help Scott.

Scott was at work in the kitchen filling up an old backpack with junk food and sodas. "I found some good boards out back," said Will, as he entered through the back door. "Did you find the hammer?"

Scott didn't answer, though—couldn't answer. He was frozen stiff. The bag of chips dropped from his hand and splattered about the kitchen floor. Will whirled in alarm. The faint sobs of the young girl were echoing from the bedroom.

Scott began to panic. "Let's get out of here and find Mom and Gramps, Will."

"They're long gone," said Will. "We'll never find them."

Scott was frightened. The crying was getting louder. "Then what are we going to do?" he cried.

Will shot a glance down at the bedroom. "C'mon. Let's find out what's going on."

The two boys inched their way down towards the bedroom and paused at the foot of the door. They stood there for quite some time, just listening, as the cries of the weeping girl sounded from the room. Neither wanted to step in first.

"Go ahead," urged Scott.

Will figured he was the oldest and summoned up some courage. "Okay, but you're going in with me," he said and with a deep breath cautiously stepped into the room. Scott grabbed onto the back of Will's shirt and followed.

Will crept over to the desk and leaned before it. He reached for the drawer but suddenly pulled back. He glanced back at Scott, who was standing wide-eyed behind him, and then back at the drawer. A determined look swept over Will's face, and with a quick lunge he opened up the drawer.

The sobbing continued, but the drawer was completely empty. Will reached his finger out and poked the bottom of the drawer. The sobbing instantly stopped.

"Do it again," whispered Scott.

"You do it," Will shot back.

"I ain't touching it," said Scott.

"Well, give me some room then."

Scott backed up to the door and watched as Will drew in a deep breath and reached into the drawer. He tapped on the drawer's bottom panel. "It sounds weird," he pointed out. "Look. The drawer isn't as deep as it's supposed to be."

Scott crept over just close enough to peer over Will's shoulder. Will was right. The drawer was only about six inches deep, but the outside of the drawer was at least ten inches in length. "See?" said Will, as he reached in and gave another good rap. As he did so, the front end of the drawer's casing popped up exposing the secret compartment that lay beneath.

"Whoa! What is that?" asked Scott, peering into the compartment.

Will pulled out a wide, flat box of dark wood. There were symbols carved into the wood that reminded Scott of the Egyptian hieroglyphics he had seen in his social studies class.

"What's in it?" asked Scott.

Will carefully lifted the heavy wooden lid.

"Necklaces?" scoffed Scott.

"No, dummy, they're amulets. See, it says so right here," Will said, pointing to a golden plaque on the inside of the lid that read, *Amulets of Acacia*.

The inside of the box was lined with dark, plush velvet. On the left-hand side of the box sat two amulets within deep grooves designed to hold them, but the indentations of two other amulets were empty.

"Where's the crying coming from then?" asked Scott.

"It's somehow coming from these necklaces, I guess," answered Will.

"Amulets, dummy! Remember?" mocked Scott.

"Whatever!" scoffed Will.

"And where's Acacia anyway?" asked Scott.

Will took out one of the amulets and held it up to the light. "Who knows—probably in South America or something."

Will turned the amulet over in his hand. It was made of a white metal that had a smooth feel to it. From it hung a dark oval stone set in silver. The stone had a strange liquid-like quality to it that seemed to swirl within the setting as it caught the light. "I wonder if these are worth anything," he said. "Gramps probably doesn't even know they're in here. Here, try it on," he said, plunking the amulet over Scott's head.

Scott stumbled back onto the bed. "What's that!" he screamed.

Before him appeared a large, silvery orb of sorts hovering within an arm's length, and with it, the sobbing continued.

"What's what?" cried Will. Scott seemed to be staring at the bureaus in disbelief, but there was nothing there that Will could see.

"Don't you see it?" exclaimed Scott.

"See what?" Will quickly reached for the second amulet and placed it over his head. The large, silvery orb materialized before him. "What the heck is that?" he gasped.

# CHAPTER 4

# *Into the Orb*

As Scott and Will moved back from the orb, it slowly followed. The height could be estimated at about four feet, its width, three, and its surface seemed to be that of a strange, silvery liquid—like the stone! The reflections of the room shimmered within and put Scott in mind of the oval mirror that was hanging in their hallway back home.

The sobbing seemed to be coming from behind the orb, Will realized, and leaned to peer behind it but there was nothing there but the bureaus. Will inched closer and examined it more closely. The crying wasn't coming from behind it but seemed to be coming from inside it.

Scott held his breath as Will slowly lifted a finger towards the orb and lightly touched it. A gasp escaped Will's lips. It felt as if he were touching the surface of water. Ripples extended out from the point at which his finger touched the orb's surface. He was even more astonished to find that the tip of his finger was actually wet!

Scott and Will stared dumbfounded as the ripples settled upon the orb. Will hesitated but again reached out to touch the silvery surface. This time, his finger actually penetrated it as if he were dipping his hand into a fish tank. It was definitely water; it dripped down his fingers and onto the floor, but why wasn't it pouring out into the room?

The boys listened in bewilderment to the weeping that seemed to be coming from just beyond the water's surface. Will tried to peer in, but only his reflection stared back at him. He inched in closer still and even tried to look in from different angles but still couldn't make anything out beyond his own image.

Finally, he crept in so closely that his nose actually brushed the orb's surface so that he could feel the cool wetness upon it. Instead of pulling back, though, he continued to press in farther and actually found himself taking a deep breath. To his surprise, he suddenly plunged his entire head into the orb.

His head was under water, or should I say—in water! He looked up in utter astonishment. He could see rays of sunlight shimmering through what appeared to be the surface of a shallow pond that his head was now thrust into. He judged the surface to be about four feet up and could make out the outline of trees and clouds in the sky above. And there, kneeling by the water's edge, was the outline of a girl, and she was crying.

Will jerked his head out of the orb and gasped for air. His head was drenched, and he was dripping all over the bedroom floor. He quickly checked behind the orb again, but there was nothing there but the bureaus and wall. "I saw her, Scott! It's unbelievable!" he cried. "It leads into a pond or lake or something, and she's sitting by it."

"Let's get out of here," urged Scott.

"I'm going in," Will announced.

"What!" cried Scott. "What if you can't get back?"

"Just hold on to my hand while I go in. You can pull me back if I need you to."

Scott wasn't so sure. "Don't," he begged. "What if it closes up or something while you're in there?"

Will was determined, though. "It'll be okay. Just keep hold of my leg."

Will took a deep breath and slowly pushed his head and shoulder into the orb. Scott grabbed a firm hold of Will's foot and held on tightly as Will continued to force his body into the orb.

The cool water swallowed Will up as he pushed farther in. With a final thrust, he drove his entire body through the orb and into the pond of the strange, new world. Scott was left on the other side with nothing but Will's sneaker in his hand.

"Will! Come back!" he screamed at the orb.

Will stuck his head back through the orb and into the bedroom. The sight of just his head sticking out from the orb was quite an eerie sight. Scott stumbled back. Water dripped from Will's head and onto the floor as he regained his breath. "It's okay," he said. "It's so weird. I can see right into the bedroom from in here. Give me my sneaker. I'm going up."

"What?" cried Scott.

"It'll be fine. Come with me," said Will.

"I don't want to, Will. Please," pleaded Scott.

Will reached his hand out through the orb. "It's okay. Take my hand," he urged.

Scott realized Will wasn't going to give him much choice and reluctantly took Will's hand. With a fainthearted gulp

Scott forced his way into the orb as Will pulled from the other side.

# *The Girl by the Bank*

The boys emerged slowly through a small patch of lily pads and took in the fresh air of the strange, new land. The pond was about four feet deep, and they were both able to stand with their heads and shoulders above the surface. The sky was overcast, and the water was cool. The pond was set in what appeared to be an ordinary green forest, and the only other person about seemed to be the girl sitting by its bank. Even so, the boys kept low as they searched about for signs of any potential danger.

"I think it's okay," Will observed. "Let's go talk to her."

"Are you sure?" Scott whispered.

"We'll soon find out," he answered and started for the bank. "Here, tuck your necklace into your shirt, just in case," he added and dropped Scott's amulet into his shirt.

"Amulet, dummy," jeered Scott.

Will gave Scott's ear a good flick. "C'mon. Let's go."

The girl was startled as the boys emerged from the water. Though her face was red and her eyes puffy from crying, the boys could see through her tears that she was beautiful. She appeared to be about Will's age, and she wore a plain dress of velvet green. Long, sandy-colored hair ran down her back accenting large brown eyes that were gentle and lovely. Will was instantly taken by her beauty.

"Oh, I'm sorry," she said, flustered. "I didn't realize you were swimming here. I thought I was alone."

Will was staring in awe. "It's okay," he replied. "We heard you crying. We came to see if you're all right."

"Who are you?" she asked. "I've not seen you here before."

"My name is Will, and this is my brother Scott."

"My name is Afton," she offered in a voice that was soft and elegant. "From where did you arrive?"

Will wasn't sure how to reply. What would she think if he told her they had come through an orb at the bottom of the pond?

"We…ah…just came from beyond the pond over there," he answered weakly.

Afton seemed to hesitate. "Are you outsiders?" she asked. She seemed unsure of what to make of the two boys who had just suddenly appeared before her.

"We're not sure," Will admitted. "Where are we?"

Afton looked a bit taken back by Will's question. "Why…you're in the land of Acacia," she replied with an ever-growing look of suspicion. "You must be outsiders if you don't know where you are."

"I guess we are," confessed Will, "but we'd still like to help."

"I'm not sure if I should be speaking with you," she responded with uncertainty. "It is an outsider that has brought evil to our land."

"We're not evil," spoke Scott, for the first time.

Afton examined the boys closely. They certainly didn't appear to be any threat. "Well, you don't look evil," she remarked, letting her guard down a bit. "You should come out of the water before you both get ill."

The boys pulled themselves onto the bank and shook off as best they could. Though it was cloudy, the air was warm. They stripped off their sneakers and socks and laid them on a large rock that sat half on the bank and half in the water. Afton eyed them cautiously. Will sat down beside her while Scott, still unsure of the strange new land, leaned nervously against the rock.

"Have you been crying because of this outsider?" Will asked.

"Yes," sighed Afton. "Because of him, I cry for my mother and for our people, but I didn't mean for anyone to hear me. I'm terribly sorry. I'm usually alone when I come down here. It's such a peaceful place."

"We shouldn't have snuck up on you like that," said Scott.

Will peered about the lovely green forest and sighed. Afton's sorrow touched him deeply, and the thought of a man that could bring misery to a place of such beauty made him shudder. "He must be really bad," Will remarked.

"He is," replied Afton, "and he's very powerful as well. His name is Dryden, and he has taken over Acacia. What was once a land of harmony is now a land of fear and sorrow. He uses his great power to benefit only himself, and he destroys anyone in his path. Late last night his soldiers came to our village and ransacked homes and set fire to our fields. He sends them often to dampen our spirits and to remind us of his power."

"Was your mother hurt?" asked Will.

"My mother was the queen of this land before Dryden's arrival," she began explaining.

"The queen? Really?" marveled Scott.

Afton smiled softly at Scott's fascination and nodded. "It is she that has the *power* of healing," she continued.

"What do you mean by 'the power of healing'?" asked Will, puzzled.

"That is her *power*," answered Afton, as if the question were odd. "What are your powers?" she asked.

Will was confused. "Powers? We don't have any powers."

"Of course you do," said Afton. "Everyone in Acacia has a power. The power comes from the land itself and is channeled differently through each person. If you are both new to Acacia, you just haven't discovered what your powers are yet."

Scott and Will stared at each other in amazement. Did they really have some type of power that was unknown to them?

Scott turned to Afton. "So, you have a power, too?"

"Why, yes," she replied, "but it's just of an ordinary sort; I can sing a melody that brings instant peace and serenity to all who listen."

That explained the beautiful and hypnotic song that came from the drawer.

"We've heard your singing," Will admitted. "It's beautiful."

"It's magic!" said Afton. "You see, though everyone in Acacia has a power, only few possess a truly potent power. Those who do are supposed to use that power to honor the land that provides their enchantments. That is the responsibility that comes with power and how the Creator has intended it to be. That is how it has always been in Acacia and should be—until Dryden arrived."

"What did he do to your mother?" inquired Will.

"Dryden is a *transformer*," Afton began.

"A what?" spurted Scott.

"A transformer," continued Afton. "He can transform people into anything he desires. It is one of the most powerful enchantments ever recorded in Acacian history."

Scott and Will couldn't believe what they were hearing.

"Let me get this straight," blurted Will, in disbelief. "You mean to tell us that this Dryden could come down here and turn us all into snails or something if he wanted to?"

"I'm afraid so," answered Afton. "It is said that he has transformed my mother into a simple water fountain, and that it stands somewhere within the castle walls that was once our home. The water that flows from the fountain is said to still possess my mother's healing power, and only Dryden uses it to keep him strong while others grow weak."

"Can he change *himself* into different things?" Scott asked.

"No," answered Afton. "He can only alter the forms of others, not his own."

"Well, doesn't anyone else have a power that can do something to stop him?" Will asked.

"There is no one powerful enough," sighed Afton.

At this time something simply incredible happened. As Scott leaned against the rock listening to Afton's words in wonder, he suddenly vanished. Will and Afton gasped in horror. A small squirrel scurried about at the foot of the rock where Scott had just stood. Almost as suddenly as he had disappeared, Scott then reappeared!

"What happened?" Scott shrieked.

"I don't know!" cried Will. "You were gone all of a sudden, and there was nothing there but a squirrel!"

But before Scott could even regain his senses, he again vanished. This time, a frog hopped about the rock before Scott suddenly reappeared with a look of complete terror on his face. "What's happening to me, Will! I want to go home!"

Will was just as shocked. This was too much. "C'mon. Let's get out of here!" he exclaimed.

"Wait!" cried Afton. "You can't go! Don't you see? It's your power!" She fell to her knees, overcome with emotion. She reached up and clasped the sleeve of Scott's shirt. There was a look of utter desperation on her face. "Don't you see?"

"See what?" cried Scott, shaken by all that was happening.

"Your power! That squirrel was you, Scott. That frog was you. You changed into those animals and then back again. You just might possess a truly potent power—a power we've been praying for."

Will was dumbfounded. "Are you trying to say that Scott changed into those things?"

"I believe so," she answered. Afton stood up and placed her hands on Scott's shoulders. "Scott," she said, "try and remember what you were thinking or doing when the changes occurred."

Scott took a deep breath and rubbed his eyes. He was still dazed. "I was watching a squirrel dart up the tree over there when it just happened."

"And the second time? Did you see a frog?" she asked.

"Yeah, I did. He's right over there," he replied, pointing to a small green frog that was poking out from under a lily pad.

"Let's try something," suggested Afton. "Try to think of some animal, and let's see if you change again."

"I'm scared, Afton," said Scott.

"It's okay," she assured him. "If you just think of yourself again, you'll change back to normal."

Scott took a few steps back and concentrated. Amazingly, his form changed right in front of their eyes to that of a great mountain lion. The huge cat leapt up onto the large rock and let out a deep growl. Afton and Will stumbled back. The great cat then started to quiver as its shape began to deform and then alter back into Scott.

"Oh, my God!" Will cried.

Afton continued, unfazed. "Now, try to turn into something else," she urged.

Scott closed his eyes. His body again began to shake before shifting down into that of a turtle. The turtle quickly pulled its head into its shell and then slowly peeked back out at Afton and Will. The turtle's shell began to waver then alter, and Scott again reappeared before them with a look of utter astonishment on his face.

"You are the one!" announced Afton. "You are a *transmutant*! You have the ability to alter your own shape. It is one of the most potent of all powers ever recorded in Acacian history. You must come with me at once. We must tell the others. You have the power to stop Dryden!"

"Wait a minute!" cried Will. "How can he possibly stop Dryden? He's only ten years old. Dryden will just turn him into a lizard or something."

"But don't you see?" replied Afton. "With his power, he can just turn himself back. Dryden's power is useless against Scott. He can then turn into a great beast of some kind and put an end to Dryden's reign!"

"No!" Scott exploded. "No!"

The thought of facing this Dryden was too much for him to bear. Scott grabbed hold of the amulet and tried to pull it off, but the necklace instantly tightened around his neck. Scott yanked again, but with each tug, the necklace of the amulet closed tighter and tighter until it was choking him.

"Let go of it!" screamed Will.

As Scott let go of the amulet, it again fell loosely around his neck.

Scott coughed loudly, lunged for his sneakers and socks, and plunged back into the pond.

"Wait!" cried Will. "Where are you going?"

"I'm going home!" Scott declared. "I don't like it here! I want to go home!"

"But you must stay!" pleaded Afton. "You were summoned here for a reason, Scott!"

But Scott didn't turn back as he pushed farther into the pond. With a quick breath of air, he plunged beneath the surface. Will quickly grabbed his sneakers and followed; Scott was still his first responsibility.

As Scott kicked deeper, he could see the opening of the orb on the far bank and quickly swam towards it. He peered into the bedroom as if looking through a window. With a hard kick he shot through the orb.

Scott landed with a loud thud on the bedroom floor. The amulet fell from his neck as he hit the floor and the orb instantly vanished. Scott scrambled on his knees into the bathroom. Reaching up, he grabbed a towel from the closet and wrapped himself tightly. The thud of Will hitting the floor echoed from the bedroom. Scott sank his head deep into his knees and cried.

CHAPTER 6

# *Return to Acacia*

Will rushed into the bathroom and over to Scott, who was still trying to gain control of his emotions. Without saying a word, Will sat down beside Scott and put an arm around him. Will was dazed as well. Neither spoke for some time. They just sat, huddled together in silence, trying somehow to make sense out of all that had just happened.

"I'm sorry, Will," said Scott, finally. "The thought of facing that Dryden was just too much to even think of."

Will understood. "I know. I don't blame you."

"Do you think I did the right thing—just leaving?" Scott asked.

"I don't know," replied Will, honestly. "Dryden doesn't sound like somebody you want to mess with, but those people need help, and it looks like you're the only one who can help them."

"But I'm too afraid, Will," Scott sighed. "I don't want to go back."

Will wasn't really sure what to say. He certainly understood Scott's fears, but he also felt sorry for the people of Acacia.

"C'mon. Let's put the amulets away and get out of these wet clothes," he suggested.

The boys changed into dry clothes and brought their wet ones down into the basement to throw into the dryer. While they waited for their clothes to dry, they went back upstairs to the bedroom to wipe up the water that trailed into the bathroom. They cleaned in silence. Will seemed to be lost in thought, and Scott was worried that Will might be upset with him for being such a *chicken*. Scott looked up to Will, and Will's opinions really mattered to Scott, but how could he ever face Dryden?

"I'm going down to check the clothes in the dryer," muttered Will.

Scott quietly followed. Will opened the dryer and tossed Scott his clothes without looking up. They were still damp but good enough—they'd be dry by morning.

Scott was relieved when Will finally spoke, "Do you think that Dryden could be the guy that Gramps got the desk from?" he asked. "Maybe the amulets were his, and he disappeared into Acacia through the orb. Two other amulets are missing from the box. I'll bet he's wearing one of 'em."

"I wondered the same—"

Will suddenly shot out like a cat and grabbed a hold of Scott's arm. "Listen!"

Scott followed Will's eyes up to the cellar door. There were noises coming from above them in the house. Scott dropped his clothes. "You don't think Afton followed us through the orb, do you?"

The thought was startling. "I hope not," Will replied. "How would we ever explain her to Mom?"

The boys quietly made their way up the stairs. As they got closer to the top step, it became certain that someone was in the house. Will paused in front of the door and touched a finger to his mouth to signal to Scott to stay quiet. Will carefully opened the door a crack and peered through. A figure swept by the door. It was definitely female.

"What do you want for lunch, Dad?"

Both boys sighed with relief at the sound of their mother's voice.

Mom was startled herself when the boys popped out from the basement.

"Oh, you scared me," she jumped. "I didn't realize you boys were home."

"What are you two doing down in the basement when it's such a nice day out?" asked Gramps.

"Well…we sort of got our clothes wet, and we put them in the dryer," Will confessed.

"Make sure you're being careful by that lake, boys," said Mother. "And make sure you clean up after yourselves, too," she frowned. "There were potato chips all over the kitchen floor when we got home."

"Sorry, Mom," said Will. He was just relieved they weren't asked what really happened. How would they ever explain? They were lucky that Mother and Gramps didn't notice the guilty expressions on their faces, either.

Will tried to change the subject. "I thought you two were going to spend the day looking for yard sales?"

"We are," replied Mother. "We just came back to have some lunch before we head out again. You're just in time to join us."

"Let's show 'em what we got," said Gramps.

Mother smiled and grabbed a lamp that was sitting on the counter. The lampshade had trains all over it. "I found this for you, Scott," she smiled proudly. "I talked the guy down to two bucks." She was obviously pleased with her bargain. "I thought you could put it on your desk back home. It'll remind you of your grandfather."

*Not trains*, thought Scott, but he didn't want to hurt Mother's feelings. Her intentions were good. "I love it," he fibbed. "It's just like the wallpaper in the bedroom. It's cool."

Scott forced a big smile, and Mother returned a larger one, pleased by his approval.

Gramps clapped his hands together. "I got something for both of you," he bubbled and took from his pants a red pocketknife. "It's a Swiss Army knife," he grinned. "C'mere and take a looksie," he said and handed the knife to Will. "It's for both of you, but since Will's the oldest, he's in charge of it."

"Cool," replied Will.

The knife had many features. There were two different-sized blades, a screwdriver, a file, a miniature scissors, and even a small magnifying glass that pulled out.

"I figured you could use it if you ever needed to cut the line or something when you were fishing," Gramps added.

"Be careful with it," cautioned Mother.

"Thanks!" Will said and slipped it into his pocket. "It's awesome!"

"Why don't you boys clean up while your grandfather and I get some lunch ready," Mother suggested.

The boys headed in the bathroom while Mother prepared a plate of turkey sandwiches. Gramps grabbed what was left of the bag of chips and got his jar of dill pickles out from the refrigerator. Both boys hardly touched their food.

Mother knew something was wrong when the boys didn't even react to their grandfather smothering his turkey sandwich in Tabasco sauce.

"Are you two okay?" she asked. "You're both pretty quiet."

"What's an *amulet*?" Scott suddenly asked. At the mention of the word, Gramps started choking on his turkey sandwich.

"Are you okay, Dad?" asked Mom, patting Gramps on the back.

"Tabasco sauce just went down the wrong way," he coughed.

Mother put some chips on Scott's plate. "An amulet? Well, it's like a charm, I guess you could say, but only magical," she explained. "Are you sure you're okay, Will?"

Will couldn't believe that Scott had just blurted out about the amulet and was shooting him daggers. "Sure," Will replied, forcing a grin. "I guess I'm still a bit tired from the ride yesterday."

"Fresh air is all they need," assured Gramps, with a loud cough. That was his cure for most things.

"Speaking of fresh air," said Will. "Would it be okay if Scott and I camped out tonight? We'd like to spend the night trying to catch Ol' Bess."

Scott shot Will a look. This was news to him.

"I don't know," Mom replied. "We just got here, Will. Maybe later in the week."

"It's okay," Gramps cut in. "Besides, we're supposed to get some rain the day after next. This might be the only chance the boys have to get out there."

Will and Scott had camped out by themselves for the first time last summer. Now that Will was getting older, Mother was trying to give him a bit more freedom, but she still struggled with the fact that he wasn't a kid anymore.

Mother hesitated. "Well...is it okay with you?" she asked Scott, noticing his nervousness. Scott wasn't so sure Will had camping or Ol' Bess in mind.

"He'll be fine," said Will. "Besides, if he wants to head back, I'll walk him myself."

"Well...okay," agreed Mother, reluctantly. She really wasn't happy with the idea, but it seemed like Will was just starting to enjoy himself, and she didn't want to spoil it. "Make sure you bring a flashlight," she added.

"Thanks, Mom," said Will, forcing a big grin.

"C'mon," Gramps said. "I'll help you find the tent in the basement."

Scott and Will followed their grandfather into the basement while Mother cleared the table. "I think I put the tent behind the stairs," said Gramps. "Why don't you see if you can reach under and grab it, Scott."

Will plopped down on an old chest sitting by the bottom of the stairs while Scott fumbled underneath for the tent. "Gramps, what was the name of that man who disappeared? You know, the one you got the desk from," Will inquired, seemingly out of nowhere.

"What made you think of that?" questioned Gramps, trying hard not to reveal his suspicion.

"I don't know? I was just wondering," Will answered casually, though his heart was racing.

"Well, I knew him, I did," Gramps replied. "His name was Dryden...Dryden Marsh. He worked for me a spell before he disappeared."

Scott and Will looked as if they had both been punched in the stomach. Will was right. This Dryden must certainly be the outsider who has taken over Acacia.

"What was he like?" asked Scott, as he yanked the tent out from beneath the stairs.

"A cold man," Gramps recalled. "Not the neighborly type—a loner. He didn't have much to do with anybody nor did he want to, I reckon. He just vanished one day and hasn't been heard from since."

"What do you think happened to him, Gramps?" asked Will, though he already knew the answer.

"Well...my guess is that he just found himself a new start somewhere and didn't bother to let anybody know about it," Gramps replied; though a guess it wasn't. Dryden always did have trouble getting along with people in *this* world, and now he's found a world in which he can control them. "The fishing poles are in the shed," Gramps said, quickly changing the subject. "And make sure you bring some warm clothes with you, too. The temperature still dips down at night."

Will reached down for the other end of the tent. "We will," he muttered. The news about Dryden was stunning.

Gramps was even more stunned, though, and paused to catch his breath at the foot of the stairs while the boys dragged the tent up into the kitchen. "Please, Good Spirits," he whispered. "Please let this be the right thing to do. If anything should happen..." Grandpa's voice trailed off. He quickly gathered himself and followed the boys up the stairs.

The boys began preparations for their overnight while Mother and Gramps got ready to head out again in search of a yard sale that Gramps had heard about on the other side of town. Though he feared that Will was really planning to go back to Acacia, Scott decided not to say anything about Will's so-called camping trip until after Mother and Gramps left.

Before leaving, Mother popped into the bedroom with some last minute instructions, "Be careful, and don't hesitate to come back to the house if you need anything. I made sandwiches to take with you; they're in the fridge. Pack the flashlight, and make sure you bring extra socks."

"Okay, Mom," Will groaned. "We'll be fine."

"Watch out for the tiger," warned Gramps. It was difficult for Gramps to kid with the boys at this moment, but it was important that he act his normal self.

"What tiger?" blurted Scott.

"Escaped from the zoo," said Gramps. "One of them Siberian tigers. Huge! Escaped two days ago—must be real hungry by now."

"Don't start that again, Dad," grinned Mother. "Your grandfather is just teasing, boys. There's no tiger out there," she assured them and gave each boy a concerned hug and kiss. "Have a good time, and make sure you stay together."

"All right, already!" barked Gramps. "Stop fussin' over these boys. They're practically men!" he snorted and reached out with both hands to tousle their hair. "You get Ol' Bess for me."

"We'll try," replied Will.

"And, boys, if it gets too rough out there, you come right home, and don't even think twice about it, yeh hear?"

There was a concern in Grandpa's voice that caught Will off guard. He wondered for a brief moment if…nah, there's no way. "Okay, Gramps," answered Will.

With that, Mother and Gramps finally headed out but not before Mother gave them one last hug and checked for their extra socks.

As soon as Mother closed the door behind her, Scott turned on Will. "What are you up to, Will?" he demanded.

"I'm going back to Acacia," he stated casually.

"But I don't want to go," said Scott.

"You don't have to go," said Will. "Just tell Mom you were *scared* and wanted to stay home."

Scott was hit hard by the insult. It was an obvious *jab* at the fact that he was afraid to go back to Acacia.

Will felt sorry almost immediately after he said it and quickly apologized. "It's just that I think we should help," he explained.

"You just want to go see Afton again," snapped Scott.

Will glared hard at him, but there was some truth to it. Will hadn't been able to stop thinking about Afton since they had left Acacia.

"C'mon, Will. You're not thinking about what could happen to you there," Scott added.

"That's not true," said Will. "I've just been thinking: I must have some type of power, too. Maybe I'm also powerful enough to stop Dryden. I have to go back and find out."

"What if Dryden turns you into a toad or something? You'll never be able to come back," argued Scott.

Though he was still upset with Will's comment, he certainly didn't want anything bad to happen to his brother.

"I won't let that happen," Will assured him. "I'm just going to try and find out what my power is. If there's nothing I can do to help, I'll come right back."

"Anything could happen, though," Scott pointed out. "What if you lose the amulet? Too many things could go wrong, Will. Please don't go."

"You couldn't get the amulet off even when you tried; it almost strangled you. I don't think it comes off until you're back, so don't worry about it. I'm going," stated Will, firmly. "You can come if you like. If not, I need you to take the tent and the rest of the stuff and hide it out back. Wait a few hours, and then come back, and tell Mom you weren't feeling so good and didn't want to stay out. Tell her I'm fine and decided to camp out by myself."

Will hated to lie, but how could he ever get his mother to believe what was going on?

"I'm not going, and I'm not going to lie for you, Will. That's not fair to Mom and Gramps."

Scott was right. This was dangerous.

"Please," Will begged. "There are people there that need help, and I might be able to help them. I can't ignore that."

Scott was stuck. He was feeling guilty about the fact that he wasn't helping these people when he had the power to help.

"Come with me, then," Will said.

Scott just lowered his head and didn't reply.

"Fine, then," snapped Will. "At least help me by hiding the tent and not telling Mom."

Will reached into the bottom drawer of the desk and maneuvered the amulet's casing out from the secret compartment. Snatching the amulets from the box, he placed one around his neck and dropped the other over Scott's head. Scott didn't budge. Will grabbed the backpack he had stuffed with extra clothes and started towards the orb. He gave a last desperate look back at Scott. "Come with me," he pleaded.

Scott didn't move—couldn't move. He couldn't even find the breath to say something—anything. Will frowned and whirled back towards the orb. He took a long, deep breath and pushed his way through the rippling surface.

Unable to even move, Scott watched in dismay as Will forced his way through the orb. With a final thrust, Will's body disappeared into the orb.

# CHAPTER 7

# Lewis & Chas

The coolness of the water shocked Will as he entered the pond through the orb. He tried to shoot up quickly to escape the cold, but the pack of clothes he was carrying kept him from using one arm. The pack had scraped the bottom as he entered and kicked up a good amount of dirt. The water was quickly turning black around him, and he was having trouble finding his bearings under the murky water.

Something unexpectedly shot by him to his right. Will whirled in alarm. Just a fish, he realized with relief, a sunfish. The fish was just as startled to come across Will and quickly darted away.

Will secured his footing on the muddy bottom and carefully lifted his head above the water. Regaining his breath, he checked in all directions for signs of danger but could only make out the natural sights and sounds of the green forest around him. There was no sign of Afton, either. The woods appeared to be calm and deserted, and it felt as if the day were much further along than back home.

Crouching low, Will crept towards the water's edge. He slowly climbed out onto the bank and scooted behind the large rock that Afton and he had been sitting by that morning and quickly changed into the dry clothes that he had sealed in plastic within his pack.

Confident that he was in no apparent danger, Will stood up and surveyed the surrounding land wondering where to begin. He had been dreaming all morning about what his power might be and was anxious to discover what it was. He really hoped that he had a power that could somehow stop Dryden dead in his tracks…then he could save Afton and Acacia.

Will decided to experiment. He concentrated as hard as he could on certain animals to see if his form would change as Scott's did, but nothing happened. He next tried to lift up the large boulder that he had just draped his wet clothes over, but it didn't budge. He even tried to leap into the air to see if he could fly—but nothing.

*Well, I guess my power will reveal itself to me eventually*, he figured, and decided to try and find Afton instead.

"If only I knew where to find her," he remarked out loud.

"I know where," a tiny voice squeaked in reply.

Will spun around, startled at the sound of the strange voice. "Who's there?" he cried, searching desperately for whomever had just spoken to him, but there was no one about.

He was about to jump back into the pond and get out of there, but the voice spoke again, "Are you looking for the girl?"

Will turned in the direction of the voice, but there was still nobody about that he could see. "Where are you?" Will demanded.

"I'm down here," the voice replied.

Will looked down and saw a long, furry, brown animal darting in and out of the rocks scattered about the bank.

"Is that you?" Will asked.

"Do you see anyone else around?" the furry animal snorted.

"Well…no…it's just that I've never spoken to an animal before," Will remarked. "Do all the animals talk here?"

"Of course we do," said the little fur ball. "Though none of you humans have ever been able to understand us before—until you. I didn't expect you to answer me."

*That must be it*, Will realized. *That must be my power! I must be able to talk to animals!* This was encouraging. Maybe the animals could help him stop Dryden.

The little creature scurried up onto the rock next to Will, stood on its hind legs, and stuck its chest out proudly. It offered Will a paw. "My name is Lewis. It's nice ta meet yeh."

"It's nice to meet you, too," Will smiled, taking the small paw in his hand and shaking it. "My name is Will."

"What brings you to the lovely land of Acacia?" inquired Lewis. "You're obviously an outsider."

"I've come to see if I can help," Will answered.

Lewis looked at Will doubtfully. "And how do yeh think you're gonna do that?"

"Do you know who Dryden is?" Will asked.

"Of course I do," remarked the creature, now eyeing Will suspiciously. "Who doesn't? He's one bad human."

"Do you think we could gather up some animals to try and stop him?"

"What are you, crazy?" blurted Lewis. "And get turned into woodchucks or something? I hate woodchucks! You must be out of your mind! You're not actually going to try and stop him, are you?"

"Well…yes. Someone has to," replied Will, trying to sound confident. "Too many people are suffering here."

Lewis shook his head. "I finally get to talk to a human, and I get a crazy one."

"I'm not crazy," Will scoffed. "I'm only doing what's right."

Lewis rolled his eyes. "I'll never understand you humans."

Will was disappointed. It seemed that his power wouldn't be enough to match Dryden's. "There must be some way of stopping him," Will remarked, though he really wasn't sure how. In fact, he wasn't sure of much in this land. He wasn't even sure what Lewis was. "Excuse me for asking, Lewis, but what kind of animal are you?"

"Boy, are you a numbskull. I'm a ferret. What did you think I was, a woodchuck or something? You better not say you thought I was a woodchuck—hate woodchucks."

"I'm sorry," Will apologized. "You're the first ferret I've ever met."

"You can't help it—you're human," Lewis mumbled under his breath.

"Hey! I heard that!" objected Will.

"I'm just kidding," snickered Lewis. "You humans are too sensitive." Lewis scurried up onto Will's shoulder. "If you want, I'll show you where that girl is staying," he offered.

Will's eyes lit up. "Yes…please. I'd really like to see her."

A huge smirk suddenly spread across Lewis's face. "Oh, now I get it."

"Get what?" grunted Will. He knew what Lewis was thinking.

"Oh, nothing," grinned Lewis, as he slipped down from Will's shoulder. "Just follow me, *lover boy*," he quipped. "I'll take you to her."

Will ignored the comment, grabbed his backpack with a snort, and started after Lewis as he scurried towards a field of tall grass. For a little creature, Lewis darted in and out of the tall grass quite swiftly. Will kept low as he followed and continued to look out for any signs of danger.

As they neared a low hill, Lewis suddenly held up. "Stop!" he whispered and pointed to a tall, thick tree about twenty meters from them. "There's somebody in that tree over there," he squeaked and quickly scurried up Will's side and hopped into Will's backpack.

"What do I do?" whispered Will, nervously.

"Be nice," shot Lewis, from the pack.

The figure in the tree swung down from a low branch and examined Will suspiciously. He was a young boy, younger than Will. He had a mop of blonde hair and appeared to be about Scott's age. His clothes were soiled, and the plain colors and designs reminded Will of the clothes that an early American colonist might have worn. He didn't appear to be any immediate threat, but Will couldn't be sure of anything in this strange, new land.

Will introduced himself. "Hi, my name is Will."

The young boy stared at him cautiously. "You're an outsider," he remarked abruptly.

"Well, yes," Will admitted, "but I'm here to help."

"My mom says you can't trust outsiders," added the boy.

"You can trust me," Will said. "I'm here to stop Dryden."

At the mention of Dryden, the boy stumbled back. "Do you know Dryden?" he asked. There was terror in his voice.

"I don't know him personally, but I know who he is, and I'm sorry about what he's done to your land. I want to help stop him."

The boy looked at Will in disbelief. "Do you have a great power?"

"Well...I can talk with animals," Will answered meekly.

The boy seemed surprised. "You're a *communicator*?"

"I guess. What's a communicator?" asked Will.

"A communicator is one who can speak with *all*. Communicators can understand all languages, even animals'. It's a valuable power," explained the boy, "but I really don't see how you plan on stopping Dryden with it."

"Well, I haven't quite figured that out yet, either," sighed Will.

The boy started to relax sensing Will's sincerity and stepped closer. "My name is Chas," he offered. "It's spelled with an *s*, but pronounced as a *z*. Where are you headed?"

"Do you know who Afton is?" Will asked.

"Of course I do. Most people in Acacia know each other, especially the *princess*."

*The princess? Of course*, Will realized. Her mother was the queen; that would make Afton a princess.

A startled look swept over Chas's face. "Your bag is moving," he gasped.

Will laughed. "That's just Lewis."

Lewis popped his head out of the bag and squeaked at Chas. "He's friendly," Will explained. "He's a ferret. He's showing me the way to Afton's. He says, 'hello.'"

"Wow! That's amazing!" exclaimed Chas. "I wish I could talk to him, too."

"You can—through me," said Will. "Lewis says it's nice to meet you."

"It's nice to meet you, too," laughed Chas. "Do you think I could pet him?"

Will asked Lewis. "He says it's okay."

Chas walked over and gently scratched Lewis behind the ears. Lewis was obviously enjoying it judging by the way he started chittering. "I guess you humans aren't so bad after all," clucked Lewis, in delight.

"Do you have a power?" Will asked.

"Of course. Everyone does," replied Chas, still scratching Lewis's ears. "I'm a *firestarter*."

"A firestarter? That sounds awesome!" Will exclaimed. "Can you show me?"

"Sure," replied Chas, proudly. He was obviously delighted that Will was impressed with his power.

Chas strode over to a tree and broke off a small branch. He came back and placed the branch on a rock near Will. He knelt by it and fixed his hand over the branch. A look of heavy concentration spread across his face. Smoke slowly started to rise from the branch, but a slight breeze came by and snuffed out his efforts. He grunted and tried again. Again, a small puff of smoke rose from the branch but without a hint of flame.

"He's more like a *smokestarter*," uttered Lewis.

"Be nice," whispered Will.

The smoke died out, and Chas turned bright red. "I'm a bit rusty," he explained, trying to hide his embarrassment. "My mother won't let me practice. She's afraid I'll burn down the hut."

"I'm sure you'll improve with time," said Will, politely.

"There have been some great firestarters throughout Acacian history," explained Chas, dreamily. "Long ago, there was a firestarter named Ignatius who could burn down an entire hut with one wave of his hand…maybe when I get older."

"I'm sure you'll get better at it," reasoned Will. "In the meantime, would you like to come with us to Afton's? Maybe your fire could help us somehow?"

Chas was unsure. "I'd sure like to see Dryden stopped, but I don't know how much help I could be against him," he confessed.

"We'll think of something," assured Will. "Come and join us."

Lewis hopped out of the backpack and onto Will's shoulder. "The girl is staying right over this hill. I'll lead the way."

The furry, little creature skidded down Will's side and continued up the hill. The two boys could hardly keep pace with him as he darted around rocks, hopped over branches, and cut through tall grass at an astounding rate. They were working up quite a sweat.

For the first time, Will noticed smoke rising in the near distance as they approached the hill's summit. From the top of the hill, Will looked down on what appeared to be a small village. It certainly wasn't modern. Small huts made of wood with thatched roofs were spread out along a single dirt road that split around a village green. Two of the huts had been burnt to the ground and were still smoking. Villagers were quietly moving about, helping each other clean up scattered rubble and comforting one another.

The village appeared to be nothing more than a simple farming community. Cows and horses were grazing about in small fields behind the huts where large gardens extended from backyard to backyard. Beyond the gardens lay great fields of corn and wheat that led out to a thick forest. Large sections of the fields had been blackened by fire, and villagers were still carrying out buckets of water from a nearby stream to douse the small patches that were still smoldering.

The stream ran through the middle of the fields and divided the center of the common where sheep grazed lazily about it on either side. Surrounding the common were buildings that were slightly larger than the simple huts that lined the road. One building appeared to be a blacksmith shop connected to a long barn. Its roof was partly charred. Other than walking, it appeared that horse and cart were the only means of transportation here.

"This is Bryce Village," said Chas, solemnly. "Dryden's beasts came for a visit last night as you can see. We're getting used to it, though," he added somberly.

*Beasts?* Will wasn't quite sure what to say, so he just put a hand on Chas' shoulder to signal that he understood. Chas nodded back and pointed down to one of the larger huts along the common. "Afton is staying in that hut over there by the stream. It's the house of Gwen. She's the Elder of the village and Afton's Godmother. I'll introduce you to her," he offered. "Afton sure was lucky she made it to Gwen's when Dryden took over the castle," he added.

Will suddenly hesitated. As he peered down over the smoldering huts, he realized for the first time that the danger he was getting himself into was real. A sudden urge to turn back swept over him, but the closeness of Afton held him firm.

"Let's do it," Will finally declared and started down for the hut. Lewis skittered up Will's side and hopped back into the backpack while Chas followed.

As they cut through one of the backyards near Gwen's hut, they came across a young girl with braided auburn hair kneeling before a washtub. A tan dress rose up before her from the tub and floated across to a nearby clothesline where, amazingly, it hung itself neatly on the line to dry. Will's jaw fell open.

"That's just Kayla," smiled Chas. "She's a *levitator*."

Lewis stuck his head out from the pack and chuckled as Will stared in disbelief. "Don't worry. You're too heavy for her," he snickered. Will smiled weakly and continued on.

Kayla was maneuvering a pair of wet pants through the air when she noticed the approaching boys. In an instant she sprang from her knees, grabbed the clothes, and rushed towards her hut. The hovering pants abruptly dropped to the ground.

"We're a bit guarded when it comes to outsiders," Chas explained.

Will just nodded and headed on, determined in his quest.

As they reached the door to Gwen's hut, Will paused nervously. A sudden tremor of doubt shook him. Scott was right. This Dryden could turn him into a toad or something, and then he'd never be able to get back. He briefly pictured himself a toad hopping around all day. He wasn't quite sure what else toads did, and he really didn't care to find out, but the thought of Afton right there on the other side of the door sealed his fate. He quickly gathered himself and gave a hesitant knock. Chas remained a few paces back while Lewis ducked out of sight in the pack.

The door slowly opened a crack. Will could make out an older woman peering out through the crack. "Is Afton here?" he asked timidly.

Afton recognized Will's voice immediately and swung open the door. "Oh, Gwen! These are the outsiders I told you about this morning! They must be here to help us!" she exclaimed.

Gwen stepped back cautiously without taking her eyes off of Will. Afton rushed out to greet them, but her smile faded when she saw that only Will and Chas were standing there. "Where is the transmutant?" she asked.

"I'm sorry, but Scott was too afraid to come," Will replied. "Only I've come to help."

Afton tried to hide her disappointment. It was Scott's power that could save Acacia.

Chas stepped forward. "I've come to help, too."

Afton smiled. "Thanks, Chas. You're so sweet—both of you are. Please come in."

Both boys blushed from the compliment and stepped inside. Lewis just shook his head, *Oh, brother.*

Afton guided the boys to a wooden table that stood in front of a large stone fireplace. The hut was medium in size. One large room served as both a kitchen and living area with a sturdy ladder that led up to a loft. There were no signs of any modern appliances, either. It was obvious that the cooking was done in the fireplace, judging by the pots and utensils that hung from the mantel, and it looked as if water had to be toted in from the stream. Most everything was roughly made of wood.

Afton lowered her voice. "The leaders of Bryce Village are having a secret meeting tonight. There are a growing number of us who are planning to challenge Dryden. The raid last night was the last straw. I told some of them of your brother's power. They're very excited. Please come with us tonight. We need all the help we can get, and the others will want to hear about your brother."

Gwen remained silent and continued to eye Will suspiciously. Will didn't blame her mistrust of outsiders, especially after what Dryden had done to the land, but Gwen finally spoke up, "Is your brother really a transmutant?" she asked.

"Yes…but he's only ten years old," Will replied.

"What is your power?" Gwen asked.

"I guess I'm a communicator," he answered, still uncertain of his full capabilities. "I have a friend with me. He's a ferret. His name is Lewis, and I can talk with him."

Lewis popped his head out from the backpack and gave a quick squeak.

"He says, 'hello,'" Will relayed.

Afton seemed impressed with Will's abilities. "That's a valuable power," she pointed out. "You must certainly be able to help us somehow. A communicator is a respected person in our land. Communicators usually serve the king or queen as ambassadors of goodwill to lands beyond Acacia."

Will was pleased that Afton approved of his power and was quickly realizing that he was ready to do just about anything to help her.

Gwen was starting to warm up to Will as well. "You two must be hungry. I've been cooking a stew. Let me get some for you."

Food sounded good.

They all sat down to bowls of stew and slices of warm bread. The stew was thick with vegetables and meat. While they ate, Afton, Gwen, and Chas entertained Will with wondrous tales of Acacian magic.

Gwen shared remarkable stories of the times when Avia, a *flyer* and Gwen's best friend, gave her wild rides across gusty skies. The memories seemed to bring Gwen to life. "I almost fell off her back dozens of times!" she gushed. "We were young and foolish then."

Chas next rekindled the heroic deeds of Ignatius, the once great firestarter. Will was certainly amazed by the feats of Ignatius, but it was the story that Afton told about a young boy named Brawn that Will enjoyed most.

Brawn possessed the power of strength, and one day, at the young age of six, Brawn had lifted a cow over his head and marched it around the common while everyone laughed and clapped. "The cow was having a grand old time," chuckled Afton. "You should have heard it *mooing!*" Will could just picture it, too, and laughed until tears rolled down his cheeks.

As they ate and shared adventures with Will, dusk fell upon Acacia, and the night air cooled. Will reached for the sweatshirt he had tucked deep down in his backpack, but Lewis wouldn't let him have it. "I'm using that as a pillow!" he protested.

Will yanked the sweatshirt out of the pack and shook his head. It smelled like ferret. Gwen watched as Will threw on a *New England Patriots* sweatshirt; she stared oddly at the clothes that were so strange to this land. Will just smiled back. How could he ever explain who the *Patriots* were—or football for that matter?

Afton lit a lantern and turned towards Gwen. "It's time," she announced and motioned for Will and Chas to follow.

Will grabbed his backpack, with Lewis resting comfortably inside, and followed as Gwen led them out the back of the hut and through a large field to the dark forest that stretched beyond. She remained a few paces in front and confidently led them along a narrow path through dense brush. Afton followed behind her with the lantern.

Will caught up to Afton. "How can she see where she's going?" he asked, nodding at Gwen.

"It's her power," replied Afton. "She can see in the dark."

Will shook his head. "I don't know if I'll ever get used to this place," he uttered.

"You ain't seen nothing yet," chuckled Lewis, from the backpack.

"That's what I'm afraid of," sighed Will.

As they entered a thick part of the forest, Will could make out the light of a fire and the faint echoes of people in the distance. As they neared, he counted at least five people that were gathered around the small fire. They greeted Gwen affectionately but at the sight of Will instantly hushed.

"It's all right," Afton explained to the group. "He's here to help us. He is the brother of the transmutant."

"Is the transmutant here?" asked a young man, excitedly.

Will stepped forward. "I'm sorry. He's not coming."

Disappointment swept through the group.

Afton quickly stepped forward and took Will by the hand. "Let me introduce you to everyone," she whispered and turned towards the group. "The outsider's name is Will, and he's a communicator," she announced.

The group sounded in approval.

With that, Afton introduced Will to each member, revealing the individual power of each. The most powerful seemed
to be an older woman named Brianna, who possessed the
ability to move about with lightning speed. Another woman,
named Dyana, had the power to turn water to ice with the
touch of a finger, while one of the men, Gillean, could actually
breath under water. It was all incredible to Will, but he didn't
see how these assorted powers could ever combine to stop a
transformer. Dryden could just turn them all into bugs in an
instant. Will didn't want to admit it, but it seemed rather
hopeless.

Gwen stood up from the log she was sitting on and with a
frantic wave of her hand silenced the group. "Something's
coming," she whispered urgently. The group froze in silence.

A pair of eyes, glowing from the fire's light, slid towards the
group. A shape started to emerge. It was a large animal of
some sort. Will was terrified. Had Dryden found out about
the meeting and sent his beasts to stop them?

One frantic cry would have easily sent the group into a
panic, but a beautiful animal suddenly appeared in the fire's
light; it was a large golden dog—a retriever—and it was
graceful and majestic. It stood proudly and peered over the
members of the group. No one stirred nor spoke. Each sat in
stunned awe of the fine creature that stood before them.

The dog spotted Will and barked. Will's mouth dropped;
the dog had spoken his name. Suddenly, the dog began to
shake, and its shape began to deform then alter. A cry
sounded from the group.

A young boy now stood before them in the dog's place.

"Scott!" Will stood up and rushed towards his brother.

Scott sighed with relief, and the two brothers embraced.

"What made you come back to Acacia? I thought you were too afraid to come back?" Will asked.

Scott just held onto his brother. "I was, but I guess I was more afraid that something might happen to you."

The group continued to stare in awe, speechless at what they had just witnessed. Finally, one of the younger members, a *wallclimber* named Gregorian, came forward, lowered his head, and knelt before Scott. "We are honored by your presence, transmutant," he declared.

The rest of the group followed his lead and kneeled, lowering their heads like knights in the presence of a king. Scott looked at Will in disbelief. Were these people actually kneeling for him? Will nodded and chuckled. "Welcome to Acacia, *transmutant.*"

CHAPTER 8

# Dryden

The realm of Acacia consists of five villages: Alden, Hadley, Bryce, Roe, and Glennon.

The Alden Village is located in the northern part of Acacia and is the largest of the five villages. Hadley is second largest and is fixed between two small spans of hills to the west. Bryce Village is the smallest and is found at Acacia's southernmost tip while above it to the east stands the village of Roe. Situated in the land's very center, and serving as Acacia's capital, is the Glennon Village. It is here where the majestic Castle Glennon rises from its precise center. It was there where the queen and Afton once lived.

The castle was once a place of breathtaking beauty. The surrounding gardens boasted flowers of every kind and color. Eden, a portly and cheerful woman, was the groundskeeper at Castle Glennon. Her power allowed her to instantly grow and care for flowers and plants of every nature, and she delighted in producing the most beautiful flowers and plants in the kingdom.

Butterflies and birds of all variety had once made their homes in the many stately trees and trimmed rows of bushes that the many castle gardeners took great pride in caring for. The surrounding grass was so soft that one couldn't help but take one's shoes off and stroll through the lovely grounds that possessed all of the beauty that nature has to offer.

The inside of the castle was also luxurious and grand. There were many masterfully carved arched windows that allowed sunlight to reach every corner of the castle, and the queen always made sure that many colorful flowers from the garden found their way into each room. The interior colors were radiant, and the furnishings were all tastefully elegant. Castle Glennon was simply magnificent, and its doors were open for all to enter and share in all that was good in Acacia.

It was considered a privilege to work at the castle. The gardeners, cooks, and special assistants all took great pride in their work and labored hard to keep the castle in tip-top condition—and enjoyed every minute of it. The sounds of workers delighting in one another would echo throughout the castle, and the queen was a joy to work for. She was quick to compliment their efforts, and she provided for them whatever they needed. In return, they gave back their very best.

The people of Acacia simply adored Queen Betania. She had the power of healing and spent much of her time attending to the sick of the land. Her very presence was said to heal one's heart as well as one's mind. She was a kind and generous woman, and she helped the people in any way that she could. Never before in Acacian history had the land been so prosperous and joyous as it had been under her rule.

❧        ❧        ❧

The day Dryden arrived was a day that no Acacian will soon forget. For many of the people, fear had never been an emotion that was deeply experienced before. There was never a reason to fear anything beyond the common mishaps of life. Throughout their history the people worked together in harmony. Their happiness and strength stemmed from their charity, and Acacians cared for and helped each other in any way that they could. But on this day the people of Acacia learned the very meaning of *terror*.

Dryden's arrival was detected just before dawn by Ogle, a special assistant to the queen. Ogle possesses a very unique power in Acacia; he is a *sensor,* one who can sense all that is happening in the land. He had warned the queen early that morning that a very powerful presence was approaching the castle. The queen had no reason to believe that it would be a serious situation, but she had alerted the workers to keep a watchful eye for any strange activity around the castle.

The first report came in just after sunrise from one of the gardeners who spotted a strange man standing in the front courtyard. He stood like a statue with fists clenched tight in defiance. An evil smirk dotted his face as he glared up at the castle. He was obviously an outsider. The queen had been quickly summoned.

Peering down at the evil-looking man from her bedroom window, the queen felt a deep nervousness for the first time in her life. Ogle, sensing the man's great power, warned her to be careful. She had a bad feeling that this outsider meant trouble, but she didn't want to alarm the others and tried to stroll down to meet him as casually and confidently as she could.

Pausing in the main archway, she drew in a deep breath to steady herself. Though her legs felt weak, she strode out firmly to meet the outsider. He was big, and his eyes were cause for the queen to stumble back; they were solid black.

The queen struggled to regain herself. "May I be of assistance?" she asked, trying to sound confident.

"Where are your soldiers?" the strange man growled. His voice was deep and gravelly.

The queen felt weak in the knees. "We don't have any soldiers here. There is no need for soldiers. This is a land of peace," she answered.

"That's too bad," hissed the stranger. "I was hoping for a little fun today."

A chill rushed down the queen's spine. It was obvious that his intentions were bad. "Why are you here?" she demanded.

He grinned down at her. "I'm just trying to decide how I'm going to redecorate," he snickered wickedly, "and the first thing that has to go—is *you*!"

A look of horror came over the queen's face as she realized her sudden doom. With a simple gesture of his hand, Dryden transformed her into a bubbling fountain that stood in her very place in the front courtyard. The change was instant. Dryden let out a hideous laugh and headed for the main entrance. Panic broke out within the castle at the sight of what the outsider had done to the queen. The man's power was obvious, and it was unstoppable.

A worker named Quinn tried to stop Dryden as he entered the main entrance. Quinn had the ability to stun people with a small burst of energy, and he actually jolted Dryden as he entered the castle, but Dryden quickly regained himself. "Nice try," he grinned and instantly transformed Quinn into another of the castle's mice. Resistance was impossible.

Dryden made his way through the main hall with large, confident strides. Workers leapt from his path in every direction. With a mere flick of his wrist, Dryden transformed two other workers into bugs as he strode by—not because they tried to resist, but for the pure fun of it.

He wound his way up to the top of the main stairwell that overlooked the great hall and peered triumphantly over the chaos as people scrambled to take cover.

"Stop!" he finally roared.

Everyone instantly froze. It looked as if time itself had been stopped. No one dared move. Dryden smiled. He was enjoying the sudden power he had over these people. He leaned on the railing and glared over the frightened people with a mocking look that dared anyone to challenge him.

One of the workers, named Marlow, stepped nervously forward. "What do you want with us?" he asked timidly.

Dryden spun furiously in Marlow's direction. Dryden's eyes widened. A slow grin spread across his face; a grimace spread across Marlow's. With a quick wave of his hand, Dryden instantly changed Marlow into a goat. Gasps filled the air as the confused goat hastened out the entrance. Dryden smirked. "Anyone else have any questions?"

No one moved.

Dryden cleared his throat and addressed the people: "My name is Dryden," he announced in a deep voice that echoed throughout the hall. "I am the new ruler of this land. You now work for me. No one leaves. If you try to defy me, you will pay. If you try to escape, I will find you and you will be sorry!"

Dryden paused to glare over the people. "If anyone here has a problem with this, please step forward, and we can *discuss* it now. If not, I'm hungry, and I'll expect food shortly."

No one dared challenge Dryden, especially after what had just happened to Marlow. Nothing could be done. Dryden was now the new, uncontested ruler of Acacia. The kitchen workers quickly retreated to fix their new king something to eat.

Afton, who had witnessed Dryden's takeover in horror from the landing above, slid down the back stairs and stole away to Bryce.

Since that day, much has changed in Acacia and at Castle Glennon. Thick gray clouds swept over the suffering land, completely covering it in a blanket of gloom. The people now live in fear and can only watch helplessly as Dryden and his soldiers come and ransack their homes and take whatever they want or need. The people can do nothing to stop him; so they keep quiet and help each other rebuild and stay strong.

The grounds of the castle that were once so lovely and inviting are now unsightly. Dryden has no taste for flowers and transformed Eden into a large briar bush that now droops sadly in the very center of the garden she once kept so exquisite. Repulsive weeds, briars, and poison ivy have grown over the once beautiful flowers and plants. The trees, that once stood so stately, have become twisted and gnarled. The white doves, mockingbirds, and swallows, which filled the castle with sweet song, are now gone, and only the flapping of great-winged bats can be heard by night.

Dryden ordered the castle windows boarded, and the inside has become dark and dismal. Rats have found the new environment to their liking and have decided to take up residence in the now foul castle. The gates have been ordered locked at all times, trapping the castle workers inside. They continue to work for Dryden only out of fear for their very lives.

Standing over six feet tall and weighing well over two hundred pounds, Dryden looks the very conqueror he is. His hair is jet-black, and his complexion, dark. It's his eyes that make him look so evil, though they weren't always solid black. It was when he first entered through the orb into Acacia that they turned to coal.

Now that Dryden has taken over the land, he delights in the power he has over these people and cares for little else. He wears a dark robe and an armored chest plate with the emblem of a black snake emblazed upon it. He demanded Vardon—the castle blacksmith who has the power to melt metal with a touch of his hand—to forge him a heavy sword with a hilt carved into the head of a snake (the first and only official weapon in Acacian history).

He sits upon a large, evil-looking throne with the grotesque head of a snake rising up from its back, and he drinks often from his healing fountain. For when he discovered that the healing powers of the queen were still present in the fountain's water, he had it moved into the Throne Room for his use only. It keeps him strong and alert.

Dryden's only companions are three wicked brothers who have pledged to serve him in return for power: Roland, Arden, and Moorland of the Blackburn Clan. The brothers are big and muscular, and their combined powers are strong. Roland has the sight of a hawk; Arden can hear a person coming from a mile away; and Moorland has an extraordinary sense of smell. As a team, they are powerful and well known for their abilities.

Before Dryden's arrival the brothers were once good members of Acacia. They lived in the village of Hadley and were respected and hard-working men. To the surprise of all, the promise of power tempted them to turn vile, as it will with some people. Now, Dryden sends them to do his bidding, transforming them first into ugly beasts before sending them out to ravage the land. They've come to find delight in terrorizing the people and keep them in constant fear as they get for Dryden whatever he desires. They have moved into the castle with Dryden to serve as his guards and are second in power to Dryden only.

Dryden, as did the queen, has also found Ogle's power to be of great value. Ogle, a short and stocky man, walks with a hunch. Though his head is oversized and his ears particularly large, he is good natured and loyal in service as the castle informer. Ogle is the only member in Acacia's history that has had the power to *sense* and has served the castle well for the greater part of his life. Though he has grown old and his power is not as sharp as it once was, he can still sense when something big is happening in Acacia. At one time Ogle was able to inform the queen of all that was happening throughout the land, and the news would always be good. But now, Ogle is forced to inform Dryden about any happenings out of the normal in Acacia or to locate those that may have tried to escape.

Ogle was now sensing something big, something or someone very powerful other than Dryden. He considered keeping the information from Dryden but feared Dryden would find out and punish him for keeping it to himself. He had no choice but to tell Dryden or pay the consequences.

Ogle entered the Throne Room where Dryden was eating dinner along with the Blackburn brothers. Dryden sat at the head of the table and was tearing into a turkey leg.

Ogle interrupted, "Permission to approach, Sire."

"I'm eating!" Dryden barked. "Get lost!"

"I think it may be of importance, Sire," he insisted.

"It better be, or I'll turn you into a chicken and send you to the kitchen. What is it?"

"Sire, I sense a powerful presence in Acacia other than yourself," Ogle reported.

Dryden dropped his turkey leg. The brothers abruptly stopped their gorging as well and turned their attention to Ogle.

"What do you mean?" Dryden thundered.

"I mean, that there appears to be another person of great power in Acacia," Ogle explained.

"What power?"

"I cannot determine that," he answered.

"Where is it coming from?" Dryden ordered.

Ogle hesitated.

Dryden slammed his fist on the table. "Tell me where it's coming from, or I'll turn you into a bug and squash you!"

Dryden's spit coated Ogle's face. Ogle sputtered. "It's coming from Bryce Village, Sire."

"Isn't that where that little princess ran off to?" Dryden snorted.

Ogle didn't answer—didn't want to answer—for his heart still cared deeply for the little princess and her mother.

"Leave us now, you little troll," demanded Dryden.

Ogle turned and left. He was now certain that telling Dryden of this new power was the wrong thing to do. The princess's life may be in danger, now, because of him. He would rather face Dryden's fury than to have anything bad happen to the princess. A single tear ran down his cheek as he closed the door of the Throne Room behind him.

"I should have taken care of that little brat long ago," sneered Dryden. "I'll bet she's up to something down there."

The brothers got up from their chairs and gathered around Dryden. "What do you want us to do, Sire?" Moorland asked.

Dryden grimaced. "I want you boys to find her. No fooling around this time. Take care of it," he added with a sinister nod of his head. "And find out about this power that Ogle is talking about, and report back to me."

With a wave of his hand, the brothers' bodies began to quiver and their shapes started to alter. No longer did the brothers stand before Dryden but three large, hideous-looking beasts. They resembled monstrous canines of a grisly sort. Their heads were over sized and their snouts were long and twisted around rows of jagged teeth. A thick tangle of matted fur covered their bulging bodies, and their forepaws were enormous and shaped more like deformed hands than paws. They stood upright in a hunched position when they walked and dropped down onto all fours when they ran. They were simply foul creatures that reflected their evil nature.

"Go!" commanded Dryden. "Go and have some fun!"

The beasts growled insanely and tore off out of the castle gate in search of the princess. Dryden's wicked laugh echoed throughout the castle behind them.

Ogle watched in horror as the enraged beasts raced into the dark forest. He knew where they were headed and trembled; he had to somehow warn the princess.

# CHAPTER 9

# On to the Castle

Afton rushed over to Scott, who was staring in amazement at the people kneeling before him, and hugged him. "I just knew you'd come," she said, her eyes welling with tears. The group erupted into joyous cheer. Scott smiled and looked at Will in amazement.

Will had never felt so proud of his brother before. He placed a hand on Scott's shoulder. "I'm glad you came," he said. "There's really no stopping Dryden without you."

Lewis popped his head out of the backpack with a squeak. Scott stumbled back. "It's okay," Will laughed. "This is Lewis. He's my friend. I'm a communicator. That's my power. I can talk to animals. Lewis showed me how to get to Afton's."

"Really?" Scott said. "You can talk to the animals here? That's so cool! Hi, Lewis."

Lewis cheeped in return.

"He says it's an honor to meet you," relayed Will.

Scott couldn't believe it. "You really know what he's saying?"

"Yep," smiled Will.

"That's so cool," laughed Scott.

Afton grabbed Scott by the hand. "Let's sit by the fire. We have much to discuss."

She led Scott to a seat by the head of the fire. No one else sat until Scott was seated. Will sat beside him. Scott couldn't believe the respect the people were treating him with. He certainly had never been treated like this before. He felt so important and had to admit: He kind of liked it.

Afton introduced Scott to each member of the group and explained to him why they had gathered. They each greeted him with warm and grateful words. There was kindness in their hearts and caring in their eyes, and Scott knew that helping these good people was the right thing to do. "I'll help in any way I can," he announced and was answered with a resounding cheer from the group. They hugged each other with renewed hope; with the *transmutant*, defeating Dryden was now possible.

Will rumpled Scott's hair. "I'm proud of you, brother."

"We must start planning immediately," Afton interrupted. "We must get to Dryden before he finds out about Scott's power."

"The princess is right," agreed Gillean. "We'll need the element of surprise if we want to defeat Dryden."

Gregorian spoke up, "Then we should set out at once for the castle."

"We can't all go," reasoned Will. "We'd draw too much attention to ourselves, and word would get back to Dryden that we're coming."

"He's right," Brianna agreed. "A small party should go to the castle by cover."

"Well, I'm not leaving my brother," Will declared. "So who will join us?"

Gregorian abruptly stood up. He was a tall boy about Will's age and seemed very serious in manner. "I will," he offered boldly. "My power allows me to climb any surface, and I may be needed to get into the castle."

The group agreed. His power would be needed. Gregorian was a good choice.

"I'm going, too," Afton announced.

"No, you're not!" objected Will. "It's too dangerous!"

Afton stuck her hands on her hips and stood defiantly. "I can take care of myself," she insisted. "I must be there to reclaim the throne. I'm going!"

The look in Afton's eyes told Will that arguing the point was useless. There would be no keeping her from going. That made four.

Chas also stepped forward. "I'd like to go, too. I know the woods better than anyone, and I can lead us to the castle without being seen."

Gillean nodded his head in approval. "If there's anybody that can get you to the castle without being detected, it's Chas," he agreed. "He's a good choice."

"That should be enough," Brianna stated. "Any more and you run the risk of being discovered. This is a capable group."

Lewis popped his head out of the bag. "Hey! Don't forget about me! You're gonna need some brains if you're goin' to pull this one off."

"What did he say?" asked Scott.

"He was just saying how honored he would be to remain in my presence," Will smirked.

"You wish!" barked Lewis.

Will playfully scratched Lewis's head. "It's set, then," said Will. "How long does it take to get to the castle from here?"

"It's about a six-hour journey if we travel through the thickest parts of the woods," answered Chas.

"Then we should prepare to leave at once."

Scott was starting to feel a bit queasy now that actual plans were being made to face Dryden, but he tried to remain confident in front of the group. They were counting on him, and he didn't want to let them down.

Will looked over at his brother and could tell that he was struggling inside. He knew his brother better than anybody. Despite their age difference, they did everything together growing up. They built forts, went fishing, and played street hockey and basketball together until they were too tired to even stand.

When they were younger, Will would save up the money he had earned from his paper route and take Scott out for a strawberry shake on Saturday mornings. Scott thought it was the greatest when Will slapped his own money on the counter to pay for the shakes, and Will loved doing it for Scott. They would usually follow their shakes with a trip to the candy store or some fishing by the river. There wasn't anybody in the world that Will was closer to than his brother Scott.

"That was some dog you turned into," Will remarked.

Scott smiled slightly. "I practiced for a while when I got through the pond. I'm still a bit shaky, but I'm starting to get the hang of changing back and forth."

Will watched with concern as Scott's smile faded. "How are you holding up?" Will asked softly.

"I'm a little scared," Scott admitted. "I hope I'll be brave enough to face Dryden when the time comes."

Will placed his hands on Scott's shoulders. "Listen," he said gently, looking Scott in the eyes. "You were afraid to come here, but you found the courage and made it here. You can do it again, Scott."

"I hope so, Will," Scott sighed. "I hope so."

At that moment, Gregorian walked over to the brothers. "We're ready," he announced.

Will looked at Scott and nodded. "You can do it," he whispered.

Scott exhaled slowly and nodded back.

Will gave him a soft, reassuring squeeze on the shoulder. "No matter what, I won't leave you."

With final hugs and wishes of good fortune, the small group turned and headed north into the thick woods beneath a bright moon. Gillean watched as the small group faded into the woods. "May the Good Spirits be with you," he whispered.

Chas carried a dim torch and led the way with Scott, Afton, and Will following closely behind. Gregorian took up the rear while Lewis rested comfortably in the back of Will's pack. Lewis was getting quite used to it in the pack and thought it rather nice to be carried around.

"I hope nobody minds, but…it's just easier this way." Scott instantly shifted his shape back into that of a mountain lion and gave a low growl of delight before falling in behind Will. Lewis stole a quick peek at the mountain lion. Scott let out a quick snort, which was just meant as a hello, but it sent Lewis diving back down into the pack. Mountain lions aren't known to smile, but this one was.

Chas had spent most of his days exploring the woods and knew them like the back of his hand. He was careful to stay away from main paths and kept to the dense parts of the forest to avoid being spied. The traveling was hard and tiring.

They continued on this way for more than three hours through a maze of forest—climbing (leaping in Scott's case) over rocks, crouching under branches, and trudging through thick bushes. The night was growing old, and exhaustion was setting in.

"We must rest," yawned Will.

Scott changed from the mountain lion back into his normal form. "I'm pooped, and the trip wasn't nearly as difficult for me as it was for the rest of you."

"I must agree," added Gregorian. "We'll need sleep if we're going to face Dryden."

"There's a spot nearby that's soft with moss and covered by thick branches," said Chas. "It would be a good place to rest, but I can't seem to find it."

"I'll see what I can do," said Will, and bent low towards a fallen log. A cricket was resting comfortably beneath the log and was busy rubbing its forewings together to produce its shrill, grating sound. Will whispered something in the cricket's direction. The cricket's song momentarily fell silent and then began again in earnest.

"It's just beyond that large tangle of a tree over there," Will announced and was met with stares of wonder. "Don't ask," he smiled.

"We'll make camp there, then," agreed Afton. "My feet are killing me."

Chas led them past the large tree, that put one in mind of an octopus, and into the mossy area. It was a perfect resting-place. The land was soft and flat, and the thick branches that surrounded the area provided good cover. Everyone just dropped as they entered. They were exhausted, and it was late.

"We can't all sleep," Will pointed out. "Somebody has to take watch."

"Will's right," agreed Gregorian. "We can't take any—Ouch!" Gregorian suddenly grabbed his backside as if he'd been poked.

"What happened?" exclaimed Afton.

"Somebody pinched me, and I won't say where!" gasped Gregorian.

"Hey!" shrieked Scott. "Somebody just pinched me, too!"

Afton suddenly grabbed her bottom with a screech. "My word! What is going on?"

As they stood there holding their bottoms in bewilderment, an old woman suddenly appeared out of thin air behind Will. She was about to pinch him as well when Will reached back and grabbed her by the wrist. "Oh, no, you don't!" he scoffed. "What do you think you're doing?"

"What do you think you're doing?" huffed the feisty, old woman back at Will. "These are my woods, and you're trespassing! Now unhand me!"

Will released his grip.

"Iris? Is that you?" Afton looked closer at the old woman and started to laugh. "It's me—Afton."

The old woman cautiously stepped closer and squinted in Afton's direction. "Afton? Well, why didn't you say so?" she blubbered and reached to give Afton a hug. The boys stared dumbfounded as the two embraced.

"You two know each other?" snorted Will.

Afton smiled at the boys. "Everyone, this is Iris. She used to work at the castle when I lived there with my mother."

"Well, what are you doing out here pinching us?" said Gregorian.

"I've been living out here since I escaped from the castle. It's the only place I'm safe," Iris explained. "What are you doing out here messing around in my woods?"

"These people are good," said Afton. "They're also powerful. We're going to the castle to reclaim Acacia. We just stopped to rest."

"My word!" Iris cried. "How wonderful! Somebody should have done something about that big bully long ago. You must allow me to put you up for the night."

They were all too tired to object. Iris led them to the far corner of the mossy area. As they got closer, they could make out a small campfire with assorted pots and makeshift furnishings scattered about the area. A wide tree stood near the fire, and its trunk had been hollowed to provide a small shelter within. The tree stood by a narrow stream, and well-worn clothes were hung to dry on several of its branches.

"It's not much, but it's home," Iris remarked. "I have extra blankets. At least you'll rest comfortably."

"Thanks, Iris," Afton smiled and gave her another warm hug.

"We appreciate this," Will said, "but how did you sneak around without us seeing you?" he asked.

"I was invisible," Iris explained. "It's my power. My years are catchin' up to me, though, and I can't stay invisible for as long as I used to, but it still comes in handy when those beasts come sniffing around. They know I'm here, but they haven't caught me yet," she boasted proudly. "Now, you all try and catch some sleep. My ears are keen, and my eyes are good. You need to rest. I'll alert you if—"

For an older woman she moved rather quickly. In one quick motion she grabbed a long stick and started whacking at the pack that Will had set by the tree.

"No!" gasped Will. "Stop!"

"There's a rat in your pack!" Iris shrieked, stumbling back.

"That's not a rat! That's Lewis!" Will exclaimed.

The old woman looked baffled. "Who?"

Lewis stumbled out of the pack like a man who had too much to drink. "What are you crazy, lady!" he squealed.

Will tried to calm Lewis down. "She didn't mean it, Lewis. She thought you were a rat."

"A rat!" Lewis exploded. He didn't take kindly to the insult. "Who's she calling a rat? She's calling me a rat? That old ox is calling me a rat?"

"Now calm down, Lewis, and be nice," said Will. "It was just a mistake."

Iris didn't make matters any better. "Are you talking to that woodchuck?" she asked.

"Woodchuck? Did she say woodchuck? I hate wood-chucks!" Lewis's eyes looked as if they were about to pop out of his head. "That's it, lady!" he squealed and charged at Iris.

Will quickly scooped Lewis up, but Lewis squirmed to get free. Iris leapt back, clenched her fists, and waving them at Lewis yelled, "C'mon, yeh little rodent!"

Chas looked at Gregorian and rolled his eyes. Gregorian just shook his head.

"Now calm down, everybody!" yelled Will. "Lewis, here," he said, turning towards Iris, "is a ferret and a very nice one at that."

Lewis stopped his squirming. "Thank you," he huffed and stuck a long tongue out at Iris.

"And, yes, Iris, I can talk to him," he continued. "It's my power. I'm a communicator."

"Well, I'm so sorry, Lewis," she apologized as she lowered her fists in embarrassment. "I didn't know."

Lewis waved his finger at Iris. "Let me smack you with a stick and see how you like it!" he squeaked.

Will ignored him. "Lewis says your apology is accepted. Now let's get some sleep."

"I didn't accept nothin'," mumbled Lewis, rubbing his head. "Who does she think she is calling me a woodchuck? She should talk—"

Will cut him off with a groan. "Good night, Lewis."

Lewis grunted and ducked back down into the pack.

It didn't take long for them all to get comfortable around the fire and give in to their exhaustion. They were too tired to even worry about Dryden. Iris promised to keep watch so they could sleep. She threw a few more logs on the fire and filled a pot with water from the stream. She had a ham bone left over from her dinner and decided to cook them a stew for the morning.

One of Iris's pleasures was a small vegetable garden she kept by the stream, and there were plenty of fresh tomatoes, carrots, and peas ready to mix into the stew. Iris searched through her garden and picked the very best vegetables as the others dozed. She filled a large basket and sat by the fire to start cutting and peeling the fresh vegetables. Suddenly, out of nowhere, a bird flapped wildly into camp. It practically crashed down next to her. It started to hop around her feet, squawking loudly and flailing its wings.

"Shoo! Go on! Get outta here!" Iris hissed, trying not to wake the others, but the bird continued its racket.

"What's going on?" blurted Scott, as he sat up and rubbed his eyes. The bird hopped over to Scott and started skipping around him, squawking and waving its wings. By this time everyone was now awake.

"What's wrong with it?" yawned Gregorian.

"Why don't you ask it, Will?" suggested Afton.

"I'll try," answered Will, and knelt down by the frantic bird. "What's the matter, little fellow?" he asked.

The bird could hardly catch its breath. "Danger! Danger!" it squawked. "Ogle sent me to warn you!"

"What danger?" Will demanded.

"Beasts! Dryden's soldiers! They're after you!" the bird exclaimed. "Dryden knows there's trouble and that the princess is somehow behind it. He's sent his beasts to find her."

Will turned white.

"What did it say?" asked Gregorian. He could tell by Will's face that it was something bad.

Will felt a lump rise up in his throat. "It's about Dryden. He's on to us, and he's sent his soldiers out after Afton. Somebody named Ogle sent the bird to warn us."

The news was stunning. Afton gasped.

"Who's Ogle?" asked Scott.

"He's an assistant at the castle," replied Iris. "He served Afton's mother."

"How close to us are the beasts?" asked Gregorian.

The bird squawked at Will.

"Not that close, yet. A castle worker named Sorrel is using her power to confuse the trail," Will relayed.

"I worked alongside Sorrel," said Iris. "She's a good woman. She must be sending strange scents into the winds. She can create any kind of scent she wants," added Iris.

"I'll see if I can spot anything," Gregorian said, and with his power, quickly scaled up the side of Iris's tree to see if he could observe anything from above the treetops.

"I'll take a look, too," said Scott. "I won't be long."

With a shudder, his body altered into that of a great owl. Iris gasped. The others also watched in wonder. With a great flap of its wings, the owl took off into the night sky.

"He's a transmutant!" cried Iris. "Then there's hope!"

Gregorian slid down from the tree. "I really couldn't see anything," he reported. "It's too dark."

"Scott's taking a look, also," relayed Chas.

Scott flew over the treetops in search of the beasts. He couldn't believe he was actually flying. He had dreamed of flying before, as most kids do, but now that he was, it was even more amazing than he had ever imagined. He darted and soared through the winds with a freedom he knew could never be experienced by humans. The speed and control in which he was able to travel was unbelievable. His eyes were keen, and it seemed as if he were looking through powerful binoculars. Though it was dark, he could still make out the land clearly. He searched in all directions for the beasts but couldn't spot them anywhere. With swift precision he turned and flew back towards the group to report.

He swooped in next to Will and changed back to his normal shape. "I traveled a pretty good distance," he said. "I didn't see them anywhere."

"The soldiers have very powerful senses," warned Iris. "Sorrel's power will only throw them off for a short while. It won't be long before they finally sniff out your trail."

Scott went over to Afton, who was still visibly upset, and placed a hand on her shoulder. She was trembling. "Don't worry, Afton. We won't let anything happen to you."

Afton's words could barely be heard. "Thanks, Scott," she sniffed.

"You still need rest, though," Iris pointed out. "You still have a few hours. You must try and get some sleep. I'll watch these woods like an owl," she said and winked at Scott.

"How are we supposed to sleep with Dryden's beasts hunting us?" asked Chas.

"I know how," said Afton, and closing her eyes, began to sing a soft melody. Her song was that of the Good Spirits, and it was more beautiful and passionate than any song that Scott or Will had ever heard before. Each note seemed to reach out to them and gently wrap about them as her voice ascended to angelic pitches and then dipped to soft, stirring tones. It was her power, and it penetrated their very souls, lulling them each into a peaceful sleep. Even Afton was able to fall asleep soon afterwards.

Iris wiped a tear from her eye that only a song of such beauty could produce and stayed up, as promised, to keep a close eye out for any signs of the approaching beasts.

## CHAPTER 10

# Attack of the Beasts

Scott rolled over from his sleep with a loud yawn. What was that awful noise? He sat up to see where it was coming from and shook his head. It was Iris. She had fallen asleep and was snoring rather loudly—some lookout.

Scott yawned again and peered over at the others. They were all sleeping soundly. The sun was rising, and he figured they'd probably gotten in about four hours sleep. He was still tired but feeling a bit more refreshed.

He almost thought of rolling back over again, but a slight movement caught his eye to his left. He glanced over and stiffened. A chill rushed down his spine. Two wild eyes, blind with rage, were staring back at him from behind a thick tree.

A sinful-looking creature that appeared to be a monstrous hound, but only much more horrid, slid out from behind the tree. Its lips were curled back in anger to reveal razor-sharp teeth. Deep from inside its chest emerged a low, rabid growl. The growl was answered by a second angry growl from Scott's right and a third from behind him. Scott whirled in horror to discover that Dryden's beasts surrounded them.

Scott quickly reached over to Will, who was still asleep beside him. "Will, wake up!" he whispered desperately.

Will awoke with a start and sat up. "What's the matter?" he grunted but gasped in terror as the fierce growls of the vicious beasts answered his question.

As if sensing danger, Afton abruptly awoke from her sleep. She opened her eyes to find the wicked eyes of a beast staring right back at her. The beast, realizing it was the princess, shot its head high into the air and howled furiously. The remaining beasts, now alerted to Afton's presence, answered in an echo of deafening howls that jolted the others awake. Lewis poked his head out of the backpack, took one look at the beasts, and fainted dead away.

One by one, the creatures rose to their full heights and began to circle the group in an unnatural, frightful strut. Their snouts were twisted in fury to reveal bone-crushing fangs that dripped thick saliva with each vengeful growl. Their eyes swelled with rage as they closed in on the group. As if by cue, the beasts dropped down onto all fours and sank their huge torsos low into an attack position. The group stood motionless, frozen with fear.

Will, realizing the beasts would make quick work of them if something wasn't done immediately, sprang into action. "Gregorian! Get Afton out of here, now!" he shouted.

Jolted from his fear, Gregorian wasted little time in responding. "Afton! Quick! Get on my back!" he hollered, and without hesitation, Afton leapt on. As she clung desperately to his back, Gregorian rushed to the side of Iris's tree. With his amazing power to scale any surface, he swiftly carried the princess far up the side of the tree and out of the soldiers' reach. The beasts howled fiercely at her escape, and with wild rage, turned their fury on the group.

The next moment was one of utter chaos and confusion as the beasts charged at Scott, Will, Chas, and Iris. There was no place for them to run or hide; they were surrounded. Scott instantly changed himself into a small rabbit and darted to safety, but Iris, Will, and Chas were trapped. They didn't even notice Scott's escape; it was all happening too quickly. The beasts were on them.

Iris tried desperately to use her power to turn invisible, but a beast made little time in closing in on her. In her youth she was able to instantly turn invisible and remain so for as long as she wanted, but she was older now, and her power needed increasing concentration. The best she could do was to fade her image, but it wasn't enough. The beast leapt at Iris and clamped down on her leg with his powerful jaws. The pain jolted her full image back. Falling to the ground, she cried out in agony as the beast tugged savagely at her leg.

Will picked up a large stick and tried to whack at the beast to get him off Iris, but a second beast vaulted at him and locked its jaws onto the stick that Will was holding. A furious battle of tug-of-war began between the two. The beast was the stronger and with a violent twist of its head, threw Will to the ground.

The third beast was set to pounce on Will from behind, but a sudden blast of flame caused it to topple backwards. Will looked up to see Chas standing above him with smoke rising from his palm and his mouth hung open in complete surprise. The second beast was startled just long enough by the blast for Will to regain hold of the stick and land a hard whack to its snout. The beast let out a wild yelp and stumbled back.

Will puffed with relief. "Thanks, *Firestarter*. You saved my life."

Chas, still amazed that he had actually produced the flame, cleared his throat in an attempt to hide his surprise. "No problem. I've done that plenty of times before."

As Will and Chas were battling the two beasts, the first beast dug deeper into Iris's leg with its razor-sharp teeth. Iris was about to pass out from the pain when a sudden flash of fur came hurtling through the air at the beast. The beast howled in pain and let go of Iris's leg. Iris struggled to drag herself to safety, but her leg was too badly wounded for her to move. She could only watch in horror.

The beast began snapping wildly at its stump of a tail. There, hanging from the end of it, was Lewis! He had launched himself at the beast and locked onto its tail with his small, but sharp, teeth. The beast kept snapping back with its powerful jaws in an attempt to tear Lewis off but couldn't get a hold of him. Lewis held on for dear life as the beast circled faster and faster in an effort to catch hold of Lewis.

"I'm getting dizzy!" Lewis squealed through a mouth of matted fur and was suddenly catapulted high into the air before landing with a hard splash in the stream.

The three beasts were now angrier than ever. They regrouped and prepared for another attack. "Keep together!" yelled Will, as the snarling beasts rose up and marched towards them.

Will and Chas positioned themselves over Iris. Lewis, still shaken up from his flight into the stream, stumbled over and dropped into the pack.

The beasts dropped low, set for a second strike. As they fixed to spring forward, an immense growl thundered unexpectedly from behind them, halting them dead in their tracks. It was so deep and deafening that it shook the very earth beneath them.

Reared up on massive hind legs stood a giant grizzly bear. The towering grizzly stood nearly nine feet in height and certainly must have weighed over two thousand pounds. It was a terrible sight. It let out another thunderous growl that sent the beasts tumbling back in surprise.

Will whirled in panic. His stomach knotted. "Where's Scott? Has anybody seen Scott?" he cried frantically, but no one could recall seeing Scott since the attack began. A sick feeling swept over Will that the beasts, or maybe even the bear, had already gotten to Scott.

Faced with the sudden challenge of the bear, the beasts momentarily forgot about the group and lunged at the grizzly. The giant bear took a quick, powerful swipe with its huge paw that sent one of the beasts crashing against a tree. The beast didn't move. Astonishingly, it changed back into its human form. There, lying motionless with one leg tucked unnaturally under him, was Moorland.

The remaining two beasts howled with renewed anger at the sight of their downed brother and charged furiously at the grizzly. The massive bear quickly fell upon them and locked its powerful jaws onto the back of one of the charging beasts while brushing the other away. With a violent twist of the bear's head, the beast was hurled into the air before landing hard by the stream. Instantly, it too turned back into its human form. It was Arden.

The huge grizzly again raised itself to its full height and roared a thunderous challenge at the remaining beast, Roland. Roland was furious, but he knew he was no match for the bear and quickly retreated into the woods leaving his brothers behind.

Will, Chas, and Iris huddled closely. They had watched the wild battle in horror. The bear lumbered down onto all fours and peered over at them. A deep growl emerged from its monstrous mouth. Panting loudly, the bear started towards them. Will reached for the stick he had used to whack at the beast and gripped it tightly before him. The bear closed in, but as it did so, it started to shake violently. Its shape started to waver and alter, and no longer did a bear stand before them but Scott!

"Holy Gamoly!" cried Lewis, poking his head out from the pack. "That was you? You just kicked some serious beast tail!"

Gregorian slid down from the tree with Afton on his back. "We saw the whole thing from above," he said. "It was unbelievable!"

Scott looked dazed from the battle. Will rushed over to him. "Are you okay?"

"I can't stop shaking, Will," he trembled.

Afton came over and wrapped a blanket around him. "C'mon," she said. "You need rest." Turning to Gregorian she said, "Why don't you see to Iris's wounds and make sure she's comfortable."

"What do we do about those men?" asked Chas, realizing that Arden and Moorland could come to at any moment.

Will grabbed some heavy twine that was heaped near the tree. "C'mon. Let's tie them up before they wake up."

The boys dragged the two men over to a sturdy tree near the fire, propped them up against it, and tightly tied them to it.

"They used to play with me when I was small," Afton sighed, shaking her head sadly at the men. "Their names are Arden and Moorland. It saddens me to see what they've become."

"Their brother is surely going to report back to Dryden," Gregorian pointed out. "What should we do?"

"We have no choice but to keep going," Afton replied. "Dryden won't stop now until he's stopped all of us."

Lewis scurried onto Will's shoulder. "No problem. Just have Scott pull that bear trick again. Dryden'll have to change his pants after Scott's done with him."

Will looked over at Scott, who was still huddled under the blanket. He couldn't imagine what Scott had just gone through. Though they saw the massive body of a grizzly bear, inside the huge beast were still the fears and doubts of a ten-year-old boy. Scott had never harmed anybody or anything in his life. Attacking and hurting those beasts couldn't have been easy for him. Will sat down next to him. "You saved us, you know," he said.

Scott was shaking. "I've never been so scared in my life, Will."

"That was the biggest bear I ever saw," blurted Chas.

"Yeah! You were unbelievable!" added Gregorian.

A faint smile spread across Scott's face. "If you had looked closer, you would have seen that the bear's knees were shaking," he said.

Will, Gregorian, and Chas burst into laughter. Scott grinned and finally joined the laughter.

"You did good, little brother! You did good!" Will laughed, patting Scott on the back.

Scott stood up and went to Afton, who was standing off to the side, lost in her thoughts. "Don't worry. We won't stop now."

Afton could only smile weakly as she struggled to stay strong.

"Let's prepare to move on then!" said Gregorian.

"Wait," Will hesitated. "We can't all go on. Somebody has to go back and get help for Iris and take care of these men."

"Will's right," Afton realized. "But whom? It can't be Scott or Will, and I must be there to reclaim the throne."

"Gregorian is still needed to get us into the castle," added Will.

Everyone looked at Chas.

"I guess that means me," he sighed. "Dryden already knows we're coming, so you really don't need me to secretly guide you through the woods anymore. I'll go and get help here as fast as I can."

"We know you will," said Will, confidently, and turned towards the others. "C'mon. Let's get ready to head out."

Before they left, Afton went in to check on Iris. Gregorian had bandaged her leg and moved her onto a patch of straw inside her hollowed tree. She was in pain but didn't complain. "How are you feeling?" Afton asked.

"Like a leftover beast pie," she quipped.

"Chas is going back to get help. He should be back before nightfall. Arden and Moorland are secured to a tree. They're not going anywhere."

"I was so scared," sniffed Iris, as the horror suddenly came rushing back to her. "That little, furry guy saved my life. Can I see him?"

"Sure," smiled Afton, "I'll go get him for you."

Afton came in a moment later with Will and Lewis. Iris wiped her eyes. "You saved my life, Lewis," she sniffed. "You're truly a brave and remarkable creature. I just wanted to thank you."

Lewis smiled. "Not bad for a little *rodent*, eh? I'm glad you're okay." Will relayed the message while Iris gave Lewis a big hug.

Iris pulled a patched blanket over her legs. "You all make sure you have some stew before you go," she insisted. "You'll need your strength."

"Defeatin' beasts has gotten me kinda hungry," boasted Lewis.

Will just shook his head.

Afton smiled. "Thanks, Iris. I'll bring you in a bowl."

Chas grabbed a quick bowl of stew and went around to hug each member of the group. He wanted to get a quick start back to the village so he could get help to Iris as quickly as possible. "Good luck," he offered earnestly. "I'll make sure Iris is taken care of, and I'll catch up if I can. You guys take care of Dryden," he said and in a flash darted off into the woods.

The others sat down by the fire and helped themselves to some stew.

"How much do you think Roland can report to Dryden?" Gregorian asked.

"It depends on if he saw Scott change into the bear or not," Afton pointed out.

"Afton's right," added Will, and turned to Scott. "Do you think he saw you change?"

Scott tried to think back. "I don't think so," he answered. "I was definitely behind the beasts when I changed into the bear, and I had changed into a rabbit so quickly, I don't think anyone saw me."

"A rabbit?" Will was surprised. "I didn't see it."

"Nor I," said Gregorian, "but bears are rare in these parts. Roland will certainly suspect that there was some type of power behind it."

"As long as Dryden doesn't know what my power is, then we're still in good shape," Scott pointed out.

Lewis scurried up to Will. "Hey, Will. Tell Scott he should turn into an elephant when he meets Dryden and do a little dance on his head," he squeaked.

Will shook his head and chuckled. "Lewis thinks you should turn into an elephant and dance on Dryden's head," he relayed.

Everyone laughed but Scott, who just sort of looked off into the distance with a steadfast stare. "You tell Lewis I've got something else in mind for Dryden," he said solemnly.

Will recognized the look in Scott's eyes. He saw it many times before when they would spend hours playing sports together. It was a look of blind determination that usually ended with Scott scoring a goal or swishing a basket. Will was starting to notice a change in Scott's manner as well. He was becoming surer of himself—more confident.

Iris' stew was excellent, but nerves kept them from eating much. They washed their bowls out in the stream and tried to tidy up Iris's camp as best they could before heading out.

Arden and Moorland were still out cold, and Will double-checked to make sure they were bound tight. With things in order, they went in to say goodbye to Iris and wish her well.

"We're about ready," Afton said to Iris.

"As ready as we'll ever be," added Will.

"One question," Iris said. "Will I still be able to get my old job back at the castle when you take care of Dryden?" she asked.

"Of course," laughed Afton.

"Then go get him!" Iris exclaimed and reached out to hug each of them. "May the Good Spirits be with you."

The sun seemed to be shining brighter than it had for some time in Acacia as they stepped out of Iris's hollowed tree. The gray clouds that hung over Acacia didn't appear to be as thick as when Scott and Will first entered the land. "We've got about a three to four hour trip to the castle," Gregorian estimated.

Scott took a few steps back. "Then, first," he announced, "some proper accommodations for the princess," and instantly changed himself into a beautiful white stallion.

Will took Afton's hand. "Allow me to help you up, my lady." He bowed and helped Afton slide up onto the back of the handsome white horse.

"Thanks, Scott," she chuckled and stroked the horse's soft white mane. She appeared every bit the princess she was as she gracefully set herself atop the fine horse, placing both legs delicately off to one side. Will couldn't help but notice how beautiful she looked. For her, he was ready to face anybody.

"Okay, Dryden!" Will cried out. "Ready or not—here we come!"

# CHAPTER 11

# Roland Reports

Darius was a young, adventurous boy of nine and had lived within the castle walls his entire life. His mother, Gemma, had been a castle worker for over fourteen years. Dryden referred to Darius as a *soldier-in-training* as he did with all the young boys of the castle. Dryden figured he could get to them while they were young and pollute their minds. In this way he could grow a powerful army that he would one day use to extend his rule beyond the borders of Acacia—and there was nothing anybody could do to stop him. Two workers were already turned into worms when they tried to stand up to him.

Darius has a bit of an odd power. He can produce a whistle so loud and shrill that it can be heard for miles away. If you were anywhere near him when he started this whistling, you'd have to cover your ears or possibly suffer hearing loss. Because of Darius's unique power, he was assigned by Dryden to man the watchtower by the main gate. His whistle was to serve as an alarm to instantly warn the castle of any immediate danger.

Darius, though, was bored with the job of gate watchman. The most he ever really got to do was just open and close the gate for Dryden and his soldiers—the only ones ever allowed to leave or enter the castle. The gates were always kept locked and guarded. It wasn't so much that Dryden was afraid that someone might get in but that one of his workers might get out.

As Darius peered out over the land that day, he couldn't help but notice the brightness of the sun; there were breaks in the clouds. He couldn't remember it ever shining so brilliantly before. He was too young to remember the times when the sun had shone even more radiantly every day.

As he took in the sun's rays, he could feel his eyelids growing heavy. The warmth felt good on his skin. He would have nodded off if he hadn't noticed a figure approaching the castle far off in the distance. He squinted to try and get a better look but couldn't make out whom or what was coming. As the shape drew closer, he could see that it wasn't human but animal—one of the beasts, but where were the other two? The brothers were never apart. The beast was moving slowly, and Darius could now see that it was limping. Realizing that something was wrong, Darius raced down the tower ladder and hurried toward the castle to report the news.

As Darius entered the main hall, the first person he ran into was Ogle, who was on his way to the castle's great library, a spot where he was often found. Ogle sensed Darius's urgency. "What's the matter?" he inquired.

It took several seconds for Darius to catch his breath. "Sir, one of the soldiers is returning to the castle and appears to be injured."

Ogle wanted to smile but kept it from showing. This was good news to him, but Dryden certainly wouldn't be happy. Ogle could sense the great power moving closer to the castle by the minute, and it was strong. He knew the princess was somehow involved and secretly prayed that she was returning with this great power to save the castle. "Let the brother in, and show him to the Throne Room at once," Ogle instructed. "I'll inform Dryden of your news."

Darius nodded and hurried back to the main gate. Ogle took a deep breath and headed toward the Throne Room.

Dryden was inside practicing his swordsmanship. He yielded his heavy sword with great power and struck massive blows to a practice dummy that was carved of hard oak. With sweat dripping from his scowling face, he grunted angrily as he struck blow after crushing blow.

Reluctantly, Ogle entered the room. Dryden instantly whirled on him with a hiss and swung his sword in Ogle's direction. The pointed end of the razor-sharp blade came to a halt centimeters before Ogle's nose. "How dare you interrupt me!" Dryden bellowed. "It better be important, or you'll feel the point of this sword!"

Ogle turned white. "Sire, young Darius has reported that one of the soldiers is returning to the castle and appears to be injured."

Dryden looked momentarily stunned. "Only one? Where are the other two?"

Ogle felt a lump rising in his throat. "We don't know, Sire," he replied. "I've instructed Darius to lead the beast here immediately to report."

Dryden growled angrily and with a quick, furious swing of his heavy sword, beheaded the wooden dummy.

❧          ❧          ❧

"The sun feels good," smiled Afton, as she gracefully slid down from the back of the magnificent stallion. "It's surely a good sign."

Scott shifted back to his normal self. "That was cool," he laughed.

They had been traveling at a solid pace for well over two hours and had decided to stop and rest under a shady tree by a cool stream. They had entered the Glennon Village a half-hour before but hadn't come across any villagers. The village was silent and stood eerily still. Word had already spread that the beasts were near, and the villagers had retreated behind closed doors.

For the first time they could see the towers of Castle Glennon rising in the distance. "We should be there within the hour," Gregorian pointed out as he scooped up some fresh water and splashed it upon his face.

"I think I still have some sandwiches in my bag if anyone's hungry," offered Will.

Lewis hesitantly poked his head out of the pack. "Well...not exactly," he mumbled.

Will glared hard at Lewis. "Both of them?"

"Well, what did you expect? I *am* a rodent, yeh know," scoffed Lewis.

"That's okay," giggled Afton, realizing Lewis's misdeed. "I don't think any of us are that hungry right now anyway."

Will took off his shoes and soaked his feet in the cool water. Lewis floated by on his back and shot a stream of water up at

Will. Will dodged it and waved a finger at Lewis. "Cut that out, or I'll have Scott turn into an alligator!" he sneered. "Alligators love ferret meat!"

"So sorry," gulped Lewis.

Afton sat next to Will and dipped her feet into the cool water as well. Lewis, still floating lazily about, sighed loudly with contentment. With a swift slash of her foot, Afton splashed water on him and quickly looked the other way.

Lewis didn't notice that it was Afton's mischief and glared hard at Will. With a sudden hard splash of his tail, Lewis soaked Will. Will shrieked from the shock of the cool water and lunged at Lewis. Afton squealed in delight as Will chased Lewis through the stream in a shower of splashing water.

Lewis, looking to escape, skidded out of the water and scampered up Gregorian's back as he tried to relax under a shaded tree. Gregorian was soaked.

"Get off me, you little rodent!" cried Gregorian.

Lewis stood defiantly on Gregorian's shoulder and poked a finger at the side of his head. "Who are you calling a rodent?" he snorted.

Scott shook his head in exasperation. He couldn't shake the thought of Dryden from his mind, and here everyone was horsing around. It was too much for him to bear. "Excuse me!" he huffed in frustration. "But do we happen to have a plan here?"

Everyone stopped what they were doing and looked shamefully around at each other. Lewis quietly slid down from Gregorian's back.

Scott spread his arms in doubt. "Shouldn't we come up with a plan?"

Afton pulled her feet out from the water and reached for her sandals. "It's really up to you," she replied. "We can only hope that Dryden hasn't realized your power yet. That way, he won't be able to plan a defense."

"Afton's right," sighed Will, climbing out of the stream. "Only you can face Dryden, Scott, and I think you know what you have to do."

Gregorian put his hand on Scott's shoulder and nodded in support as Scott looked up at him.

Scott looked pale but took a deep breath. "Okay, then. Let's do it."

❦        ❦        ❦

Darius led Roland into the Throne Room. Roland was still in the form of a beast and looked weary and defeated from the battle. Dryden immediately transformed him back into his human form. "Drink from the healing fountain," he demanded, "then tell me what's going on."

Roland panted as he dragged his left leg over to the fountain. He scooped up some water and drank eagerly. The change was incredible—instant. His color immediately returned, his leg healed. Feeling renewed, his anger returned as well. "Arden and Moorland have been captured," he grunted.

Dryden's eyes bulged with rage. "Captured? How?"

"We had the princess in our reach when a great bear appeared out of nowhere," Roland explained. "The bear was too powerful. We were no match for it." Roland shook his head in disbelief. "There certainly had to have been some power behind that creature, Sire."

Dryden scowled and furiously paced back and forth pondering the news. "Who was with the princess?" he sneered.

"I recognized most of them," Roland answered. "They're mostly a young bunch. One was a wallclimber from Bryce Village. He shot up a tree with the princess on his back," he grumbled. "That old hag Iris was there too." A smirk spread across his face. "Arden caught up with her, though." He grinned wickedly before his scowl returned. "There was a young firestarter there from Bryce as well. He gave me a pretty good burn," he huffed. "There was another, though, that I did not recognize—a boy. His clothes were peculiar; he didn't appear to be from these parts. I'm not sure what his power is, but he seems to be traveling with a weasel, a crazy little critter—took a nasty bite out of Arden's tail."

"Are you sure that was all?" snarled Dryden.

"The bear was the only other thing I saw," he replied, for Roland never did catch sight of Scott. Roland had been circling around the back of the group when Scott had first awoken that morning to spot Moorland staring back at him from behind a tree. Roland was the first to spot the princess and had kept his eyes glued to her as Gregorian whisked her to safety. Scott had then changed into a rabbit and disappeared before Roland and his brothers had turned their attention back to the group.

Dryden scowled. "It must be this unknown boy who has the power," he muttered, referring to Will, and turned on Ogle. "What power might this boy have that can explain the bear?" he demanded.

Ogle sensed that there was something Roland had missed, but he didn't want to help out any more than he had to. He didn't dare say what he was really sensing. *Could it be likely?* A *transmutant* was a power of legend. "I believe the boy may be a communicator," said Ogle. "He may have simply asked the bear to help him."

"Bears aren't the sort to bother with people," remarked Roland. "A communicator doesn't seem likely."

"What else, then?" barked Dryden.

Ogle tried to throw Dryden further off the mark. "He could be a *beastmaster*," suggested Ogle, though he sensed that this was not what the power was. "Beastmasters have the power to control animals," he added. "That might also account for the little animal that Roland saw with the boy."

Dryden seemed to accept this and laughed. A beastmaster wouldn't pose him any real threat. "So we've got ourselves a beastmaster coming for a little visit, eh?" Dryden snickered. "I can't wait to see his face when I turn his bear into a furry, little puss."

Smiling arrogantly, Dryden turned to Darius. "Get out to the gate. When our guests arrive, tell them I'd like to have them for lunch." He then turned to Roland and smirked. "Of course, I'll turn them into chickens first. I just love chicken!"

❦     ❦     ❦

Afton gasped when the castle finally came into full view. She hadn't seen it in some time and couldn't believe how run-down and horrible it had become. Where were the beautiful gardens she remembered? The soft, luscious grass? The sounds of birds singing and the merriment that would echo throughout the castle?

Thorns and briars now climbed through twisted trees and up rotting walls. Windows were boarded shut, and a gloomy silence hung over the place.

Lewis poked his head out from the backpack. "That's the place we fought beasts to save?" he snorted. "You gotta be kiddin' me."

Will was also surprised. This wasn't quite what he expected, either. It looked like one of those old, ruined castles he'd seen pictures of in his social studies book. He didn't know what to say, so he just placed a hand on Afton's shoulder to let her know he understood. He couldn't imagine the pain she felt.

Gregorian had visited the castle only once before, when he was much younger, and though he couldn't remember much, he did remember the awe he felt at its magnificence. He shuddered at the thought of the evil that could have done this.

Similar thoughts raced through Scott's mind as he peered over the ungodly-looking castle. His knees were feeling weak. He knew the time was drawing near when he would have to face the man that had created this evil.

Moving on, they ducked behind a large cluster of bushes that stood about fifty meters from the castle.

"Stay low while I check things out," Scott instructed and instantly changed himself into a small blue bird. He thought about changing into a hawk or an eagle but figured that those magnificent creatures might draw unwanted attention. Who would notice a harmless blue bird? He darted off towards the castle.

He couldn't generate the same power as he could with the wings of the owl, but the delight of flying was no less. He wished Will could experience this joy, also. He didn't think he could ever describe the experience in words.

Scott circled the main gate to see what they were up against. As he swooped down closer, he was surprised to see that the watchtower was empty. In fact, there was nobody about. The place seemed to be deserted. What good fortune, he thought, and immediately flew back to report the good news.

Will was surprised. "There's no one in the watchtower?"

"Maybe Dryden feels he doesn't need a lookout," Gregorian remarked.

"But he knows we're coming," Afton pointed out. "Don't you think he'd be watching out for us?"

"Let's hurry, then," urged Scott. "Maybe we've just arrived at a good time."

"Perhaps, but stay alert," cautioned Will. "It could be a trap."

The group crouched low and made a quick dash for the castle wall. They ducked behind a large, twisted tree that was tangled up against the far end of the wall.

"Stay as close as possible to the wall, and make your way towards the main gate," Gregorian whispered. "I'm going over. Hopefully, I can get you in. If you don't hear from me in ten minutes, you can assume I was captured." With that, Gregorian quickly slid up and over the side of the wall with the grace of a giant spider.

With their backs to the wall, Scott, Afton, and Will crept towards the gate. "Keep your eyes peeled for any traps," Will warned.

Lewis poked his head out of the backpack. "Do we have to go in this place? It looks creepy in there," he squeaked. "Maybe we could just ask Dryden to come out."

Will gently hushed him, "Sssh…stay low. We have to surprise Dryden. It's the only way."

Lewis ducked into the pack. "I'll be in here, then."

They inched their way along the mossy wall, edging closer to the castle gate. Seconds felt like minutes as they carefully dodged twisted limbs of gnarled trees, avoided overgrown briar bushes, and ducked under great thorned branches. As they closed within fifteen meters of the gate, they made a final dash for a large thorn bush sprouting crudely by the gateway.

"We should wait here," instructed Will. "We'll give Gregorian five more minutes."

Crouched low, they held their breaths and waited.

Will peered over at Scott. He could tell that Scott was nervous. The time was drawing near when all would rest in his hands. Will leaned towards him. "If we don't hear from Gregorian soon, it'll be up to you to get us in the castle," he whispered.

Scott just closed his eyes and nodded.

Suddenly, the main gate groaned in agony and slowly began to grind open. They could only hope that it was Gregorian on the other side. If not, the battle would begin right there and then. Will turned to Scott. "Be ready."

Will tried to peer into the opening, but it was too dark. A hushed voice called from the other side, "Quick! There's no one around!"

Scott exhaled in relief. "It's Gregorian. C'mon. Let's go."

Will grabbed Afton's hand and followed as Scott lead them through the main gate and into the very courtyard where Dryden had first stood two long years before. The courtyard was even more overgrown and tangled than the outside of the castle. Afton looked around in horror. It seemed like it was just yesterday that she and her mother had strolled through this once lovely courtyard trying to name the beautiful flowers that Eden had graced the court with. Ugly weeds had now replaced them, completely covering the now cracked and broken slates of the court.

"There's an entrance to the storage room around the side," whispered Afton. "We should be able to get into the castle through there."

Without wasting time, they scooted around to the side entrance. Afton was right: It was unlocked. Will still couldn't believe they were able to get inside the castle as easily as they did. "Stay alert," he warned. "I still think it's strange there's nobody about. We could be walking right into the middle of a trap without knowing it."

Cautiously, they opened the side door and slid into the castle. Just as Gregorian closed the door to the service entrance behind him, young Darius emerged from the castle's main entrance and headed back to the watchtower. He had just missed the group slipping through the gate by a matter of seconds.

The group had actually arrived at the castle not long after Roland, who had traveled back slowly because of his injured leg. It was nothing but a stroke of pure fortune that Darius was still in the Throne Room when the group had arrived. The Good Spirits were definitely with them. The gate had only been left unguarded for a matter of minutes.

Darius climbed the tower and peered out over the land anxiously. He stood up as straight as he could, raised his shoulders, and stuck out his chest and bellowed: "Halt! Who goes there?"

He wanted to be ready when the *rebels* finally arrived. He practiced again using a lower voice. He was excited to finally be getting some action.

# CHAPTER 12

# Showdown!

Sliding through the side door, the group found themselves in a deserted room that was used for food storage. The room was musty, and cobwebs of every size covered dusty shelves of pre- servatives and tall pyramids of stout grain barrels that were stacked about on the hard stone floor. It seemed the room was a favorite of the castle mice.

Lewis hopped onto Will's shoulder. "This place smells!" he squealed.

"What did he say?" asked Afton.

Will hesitated. "Ah…he says he's eager to get this over with."

Lewis put his hands on his hips. "I said, it smells, Mister communicator. S-M-E-L-L-S! As in stinks!" he barked. "Some communicator you turned out to be."

Will ignored him.

Scott stepped forward as if the weight of the world were resting upon his shoulders. "I should go on alone from here."

"What?" cried Will. "No way! I'm not leaving you!"

"I don't want anything to happen to you, Will," Scott replied.

"Then don't let anything happen to me," said Will, firmly. "I'm going."

Scott could see in Will's eyes that there was nothing he could say that would keep Will from following. "Nobody else, then," Scott insisted. "There's no use putting everybody in danger."

"Well, I'm going, too!" declared Afton.

Gregorian gently placed a hand on her shoulder. "Scott's right. Only he can face Dryden. We've done all we can possibly do at this point. We should stay behind."

Afton just lowered her head. She knew that going along might hinder Scott more than help him.

"Where might Dryden be at?" Will asked Afton.

"I would think the Throne Room on the second floor," she replied. "Those stairs over there will lead you up to the main hall," she said, pointing to narrow stone steps on the far end of the room. "The Throne Room is located on the landing at the top of the main stairwell."

Will looked at Scott. A lump rose in his throat. "Are you ready?"

Scott exhaled deeply and nodded.

"Wait!" cried Afton, as she rushed over to Will and Scott. "Please be careful," she urged and hugged them both firmly.

Will reached out and wiped a lone tear from her eye. "We'll see you in a bit. I promise."

The boys turned and started for the stairs. Feeling helpless, Afton turned away as the boys disappeared up the narrow steps. Gregorian simply embraced her.

❧     ❧     ❧

Gregorian led Afton over to a dusty chair and wiped it off so she could sit. The only thing they could do now was wait, so Gregorian pushed a large box from the corner over towards Afton to rest upon. As he neared, a sharp clicking sound stopped him dead in his tracks. Afton gasped. A door at the front of the room was slowly creaking open. Somebody was entering the storage room, and there was no time to hide. Gregorian grabbed a loose board from the floor and prepared to use it. Afton held her breath.

As the door squeaked open, a large head with big ears poked out from behind it. "Afton? Are you in here?"

It was Ogle. Afton was overcome with joy to see him and rushed to hug him. "Oh, Ogle! It's so good to see you, but how did you know we were here?"

Ogle was misty eyed. "I could sense your presence, little one. Oh, how I missed you."

They embraced as old friends will who haven't seen each other in some time. Ogle looked up from his embrace to notice Gregorian standing there. "Is that you, Gregorian? My, how you've grown since I last saw you!" Ogle looked down at the board in Gregorian's hand. "I hope you're not planning on striking me with that."

Gregorian blushed and tossed the board aside. "Sorry, Ogle. I didn't realize it was you. It's good to see you again, too."

Afton looked up at Ogle anxiously. "Where's Mother? Is she back?"

Ogle lowered his head. "Dryden had her moved into the Throne Room. She still remains in the form of a fountain."

Afton sank her head into Ogle's shoulder. She missed her mother more than words could explain.

A thunderous crash suddenly brought the happy reunion to an abrupt halt. The door had been dislodged from its hinges. Afton, Ogle, and Gregorian stumbled back in terror. Standing there, fit to kill, was Roland. His eyes were red and bulging, his nostrils flaring with anger. His face was blanketed in a hideous scowl. He lunged at Ogle and grabbed hold of his collar. "I knew you were up to something, you little dwarf!" he hissed and lifted Ogle high into the air before tossing him back to the ground. Ogle landed with a thud on the cold stone floor. Roland swiftly turned on Afton. "This time, you won't get away!" he growled and lurched towards her.

Gregorian quickly threw himself between Afton and Roland but was no match for the huge man. Roland stood more than a head taller and had arms as thick as tree trunks. With a hard shove Roland hurled Gregorian into a stack of grain barrels. Grain spilled everywhere as the barrels came crashing down upon him. He scrambled to get up, but one of the barrels had struck him hard on the leg. He couldn't move it.

"Leave her alone!" Gregorian yelled as he desperately squirmed in the grain to get up. Reaching up blindly, he caught hold of Roland's ankle, but Roland, without even so much as looking down, brought the heel of his boot down hard into Gregorian's stomach and continued on towards Afton.

Afton was trapped in a corner with no way of getting out. Her back was to the wall, and tall stacks of grain barrels surrounded her. Roland grinned as he closed in on her. "Where's your little bear now?" he laughed and reached out to grab her. Afton tried to dodge him to the right, but Roland was too quick and caught hold of her arm. She cried out in pain as Roland, who was now laughing uncontrollably, wrenched her arm behind her back.

Just then, blasts of flame shot out of nowhere and caught Roland on the backside. With a loud yelp, Roland let go of Afton and started to whack frantically at his bottom. He whirled around in fury. Smoke bellowed from the back of his scorched pants. Standing defiantly in front of him was Chas!

"One more move, and I'll fry your buns!" roared Chas.

Roland was so startled he stumbled back into a stack of grain barrels. The huge barrels came crashing down upon him, knocking him unconscious.

"Way to go, Chas!" yelled Gregorian.

Afton tried to regain her breath. "Thank the Good Spirits you came back!"

Ogle, moving slowly and favoring his right shoulder, helped Gregorian onto the chair. Gregorian smiled in wonder. "How did you get back so quickly, Chas? You're supposed to be getting help for Iris."

"Well, instead of heading all the way back to Bryce," Chas explained, "I headed to Brianna's hut just west of Iris's camp. She was at the secret meeting, so I knew she'd help. Brianna sent her son Jonus to guard Arden and Moorland and went back herself to get help from the village. I got here as fast as I could, and it looks like it was a good thing I did."

"It sure was," sighed Afton, "but how did you get through the main gate?"

Chas's face abruptly turned red, and his feet started to shuffle about nervously. "I didn't mean any disrespect towards the castle, but…I'm afraid you're going to need a new gate, Afton. It's a little charred right now," he sputtered. "It couldn't be helped, though. Darius was in the watchtower when I got there—we used to play together when we were small. I told him if I heard one peep of that whistle of his, I'd bake his bottom. Darius threw his hands up in the air, yelled he quit, and stormed off. The gate was still closed. There was no other way in."

Afton tried not to laugh but couldn't help it. The others joined in the laughter.

❦          ❦          ❦

Scott and Will stopped at the top of the stairs leading from the storage room and scanned the main hall. It was musty and dimly lit by torches. Small chittering mice, protesting the boys' invasion, darted from corner to corner. A few workers passed through the hall but kept to themselves and spoke only in whispers when necessary. Scott figured they did so because they didn't want to attract Dryden's attention in any way should he happen to be near—a horrible way to live.

"C'mon. They won't even notice us," said Will. "We can make our way around the wall to the stairwell."

Scott followed as Will cautiously stepped into the hall and crept through the shadows to the bottom of the winding staircase. Will was right: Not one worker even lifted a head to look up at them as they passed. Scott thought it rather eerie.

They paused at the bottom of the stairwell and peered up the dark, winding stairs. The stairway seemed to climb endlessly. "That must be the Throne Room up there," said Will, pointing to two massive doors that stood in the center of the landing.

Lewis poked his head out from the pack and looked up at the enormous doors. "Let me know when it's over," he grimaced and ducked back down into the backpack.

Scott's heart started to race. His knees felt weak; he hesitated. "I'm scared, Will."

Will closed his eyes and steadied himself. He had to stay in control for his brother's sake. "Me, too," he admitted. "But you can do it," he said, looking Scott squarely in the eyes.

Scott's stomach was queasy. He grabbed hold of the railing and leaned on it for support. He pulled himself up each stair as he headed for the landing, his eyes never once parting from the massive doors of the Throne Room. He kept waiting for the doors to slam open and for Dryden to rush out, but they remained threateningly still.

Will paused on the top stair and reached for Scott's shoulder. "Remember, no matter what happens, I won't leave you."

Scott tried to gain control of his emotions. "Will...well...if anything should happen, I...just wanted you to know...you know."

Will embraced Scott. He did know. Scott's hug said what he couldn't express in words.

Scott took a deep breath. "Let's go meet Mr. Marsh."

The boys inched their way to the great doors. It seemed to Scott as if they were moving in slow motion. Dwarfed by the sheer size, they paused under the doors' archway. "What now?" asked Scott.

Lewis poked his head out of Will's backpack. "Why don't you knock?"

"Why don't you just get back into the pack," snapped Will.

"You got a better idea?" squawked Lewis. Will just stared blankly at the doors. "I didn't think so," Lewis grunted and sank back down into the pack with a loud snort.

Will exhaled and reached out to grab hold of one of the thick brass handles. He pulled hard, but the door barely budged. Scott grabbed hold as well, and they pulled with all their might. With a deafening moan, the door slid open. A dank, musty odor immediately filled their nostrils, forcing them to block their noses.

The room was pitch black, but as their eyes adjusted to the blackness, they could slowly start to make out the features of the room. The ceiling was high, the space immense. The floor-to-ceiling windows were boarded shut and covered with a thick black material that rustled from the wind howling through the windows' many cracks. From each of the corners hung wavering torches, but they were hardly enough to light the large area.

On the right side of the room lay a great table the length of the hall. Four hulking chairs were clustered at the far end. Statues of the Great Saints lined the wall to the left, which cast threatening shadows throughout the room in the flickering torchlight. Cobwebs of tremendous size hung from every fixture and corner of the room.

Scott jumped back as something swooped down from overhead. "It's just a bat," gasped Will.

A great rustling of wings suddenly echoed throughout the room from high above. Scott and Will looked up to see the outline of hundreds of enormous bats hanging from the hall's rafters. "This place is horrible," winced Will.

Scott abruptly seized Will's arm. "Don't move. Somebody's over there," he gasped.

Will whirled in terror, expecting Dryden to rush them, but the figure remained hauntingly still. A sigh of relief escaped Will's mouth as his eyes adjusted on the figure. It wasn't a person at all but a wooden dummy with huge gouges in it. The head was missing.

Scott kept hold of Will's arm as they inched farther into the dark room. Their eyes were now growing accustomed to the dark, and they could start to make out the far end of the hall. In the far-left corner a white fountain, which seemed so clean and pure, stood in stark contrast to the dark and evil room. Next to it, high up on a large platform, stood a large throne with the head of a snake rising up from its back. There appeared to be no one else in the room.

"It doesn't look like he's in here," whispered Scott, but the boys were not so lucky, for there, sitting silently in the shadows upon his throne, was Dryden. He had sat perfectly still and watched quietly as the boys fumbled their way into the room. He knew they would soon arrive and had snuffed out most of the inner torches in anticipation. He sat confidently with his arms resting upon the great arms of the throne. His was the face of pure evil.

Noticing him in the same instance, the boys grabbed hold of each other with loud gasps and stumbled back in terror.

Dryden's black eyes bore through them. "Welcome, my guests," he hissed in a voice that sounded like that of a demon. "I've been expecting you."

Scott and Will stood frozen, trembling in fear. Dryden was even more terrible than they had ever imagined.

Dryden grinned at the sight of the cowering boys. "So, you've come to save Acacia, have you? Which one of you, may I ask, is the great *beastmaster,* and where is your dancing bear? I was hoping for a little entertainment today."

*A beastmaster? Dryden doesn't know what Scott's power is,* Will realized. *He thinks it was a beastmaster that controlled the bear that attacked his soldiers. He has no idea that the bear was actually Scott!*

With renewed hope, Will stepped forward. "What you've done here is wrong, Dryden. You had no right to take over this land."

Dryden scowled down at Will. "Are you going to stop me, *Mr. Beastmaster*? Huh? Is your big, bad bear going to jump out at me?" Dryden shot up from his throne. His eyes bulged with anger. "You could come in here with a hundred bears, and it would make no difference. I'd turn them all into ants and let my pets feed." Dryden arrogantly sat back down as the bats rustled from high above.

Dryden stared at the boys as if he were pondering the answer to a riddle and leaned forward. "What insect would you like to become?" he smirked. "A little beetle? A cockroach? Maybe I should just let my winged friends decide. They haven't eaten in a while."

The very thought made Will gasp in horror. He tugged at Scott's sleeve. "Scott, now!" he yelled, "Do something!"

But Scott didn't respond. He was too terrified to even move.

Dryden grinned and shook his head. "Nice try, Beastmaster," he said, and with a flick of his wrist, Will disappeared.

Will's backpack hit the floor with a thud, and Lewis tumbled out. A small beetle scurried under the hall's long table.

Lewis was stunned. "Will!" he squealed. "What did he do to you?"

Just as suddenly, a huge bat tore out of the ceiling towards the beetle. Lewis threw himself at the huge bat and knocked it away just before it could grab its meal. The bat regained its balance and swooped down again, this time, followed by a second hungry bat. Lewis stood his ground and swung wildly at the attacking bats, keeping them from snatching up the beetle that was Will. They circled for another attempt. Lewis braced himself over the helpless beetle. "C'mon!" he yelled at the hungry bats, waving his fist in the air. "I'll knock yeh into tomorrow!"

Horrified at Will's disappearance, Scott was jolted from his trance with a scream of horror that echoed throughout the castle: "Will!"

Dryden chuckled.

Scott glared hard at him. "No more!" he roared and with clenched fists started towards Dryden.

Dryden didn't even flinch. He found it all amusing. He just grinned at Scott and flicked his wrist as if merely flicking dust off of his sleeve. Scott vanished instantly, transformed by Dryden into that of an ant. Dryden laughed loudly, "Silly boys."

Scott instantly reappeared and continued walking steadfast towards Dryden. "I said, no more!" Scott vowed in fury.

Dryden was momentarily stunned. He sprang up from his throne and viciously flicked his wrist again at Scott. For a second time Scott was instantly transformed into an ant but, just as quickly, reappeared without missing a step. "It's over, Dryden!" Scott roared louder still as he closed in on the stunned transformer.

"What is this?" cried Dryden, turning pale. He gave his hand another frantic wave that again turned Scott back into the small black ant and waited. Dryden watched anxiously as the ant scampered towards him. Seconds went by—a minute. Convinced that the young boy wouldn't reappear again, Dryden finally let out a deep breath and sank back down into his throne. *Strange*, he thought. *What had happened?*

He glimpsed down at the tiny ant that was still inching towards him and shook his head. A smile slowly spread across his face. Finally, he broke into uncontrollable laughter and raised a foot to stamp out the bothersome ant.

In a sudden flash of bright orange, black, and white, a great beast sprang up at Dryden from the spot in which the ant had been. Dryden gasped. A monstrous tiger materialized just centimeters before him. The ferocious cat peered into Dryden's bulging eyes. Its hot breath stormed across Dryden's face. With an ear-splitting roar the massive tiger pounced on Dryden. A horrifying scream echoed throughout the castle.

Hideous cries filled the hall as the tiger attacked. With maddening shrieks the hundreds of great-winged bats took to flight, darting in a frenzy throughout the hall. The immense tiger continued its savage assault with enraged and deafening roars. The scene was horrifying, and the awful noises that emerged from the room were enough to send chills down the bravest of backs.

With a final, resounding roar Dryden's screams abruptly stopped. At that very moment, the bats tore out of the room through a hole in the ceiling leaving the room eerily quiet.

# CHAPTER 13

# *Wherein All That's Good Returns*

Scott sank to his knees in grief and cried out his brother's name. Dryden would threaten Acacia no more, but it had cost Scott his brother. Will was gone, transformed into a beetle, and it was Scott's fault. If he had only acted sooner, Will would still be with him. Burying his face in his hands, Scott sobbed uncontrollably for what seemed like hours, though it was really but minutes. He just wanted his brother back.

Scott was rocking back and forth when a weak voice called out to him, jarring him from his misery, "Scott?"

Scott's head shot up from his knees. "Will? Is that you?"

He whirled around to find Will on his knees trying to steady himself under the hall's great table. Scott screamed out to his brother and raced to his side. His tears turned to those of relief and joy as he helped Will into a sitting position. "I thought I lost you, Will. I was so scared."

"I'm okay," Will coughed and reached out to hug his weeping brother. They held onto each other as people will who have survived a great ordeal together. Will gently pulled away and let out a deep breath. "I guess now that Dryden's gone, his power over everything is gone, too. You did it, Scott. It looks like it's over."

"I hope so," sobbed Scott. He just wanted to forget about the horrible scene.

Will got to his feet and looked around the ravaged room in disbelief. His head was still spinning as he gazed over the destruction. "Where's Lewis?" he asked and whirled around in a quick, desperate search for his brave friend. He spotted Lewis lying still by the far leg of the table. Blood matted his fur. Lewis had fought several bats away from Will, attack after attack. In the end the bats had turned on Lewis.

Will rushed over and kneeled beside his little friend. "He saved my life," he whispered in an effort to hold back tears.

Just then, Afton and Ogle rushed into the dark room. Ogle immediately started tearing the black material from the windows. They had listened in horror to the ghastly cries echoing from the room and immediately rushed up after it had all ended so abruptly. As Ogle cleared each window, rich golden sunlight pierced its way through every crack, completely flooding the room in forgotten sunshine.

Afton cried out and dashed to the back of the room. There, lying near the back wall where the fountain had once stood, was an older woman. She appeared to be unconscious.

Afton rushed to the women's side and scooped her up in her arms. The woman slowly opened her eyes and looked up to a face that looked much older than she knew it to be. "Afton? Is that you? What has happened?"

Tears of joy raced down Afton's cheeks. "It's okay, Mother," she whispered. "You're safe now."

❧          ❧          ❧

Eden found herself lying in the middle of the garden where she had unknowingly drooped as a briar bush for the past two years. She shook her head briskly in an attempt to regain her senses. She wondered how long she'd been asleep.

She pulled herself to her feet and peered around at her surroundings. What she saw jolted her out of her daze. Her beautiful garden was now overgrown with weeds and ivy! "Goodness gracious!" she shrieked. "What has happened here?" She spun in a tizzy. "Where are my workers?" she cried. "Where are my workers? We've got work to do! We've got work to do!"

Quinn, who had spent the last two years as a castle mouse, was wobbling on his hands and knees in a state of disarray by the main entrance. Two other workers, Kern and Kora, who had both spent their time as bugs, sat stunned to his right. Nearby workers rushed to help them to their feet.

Quinn gasped as he looked around the dreadful main hall for the first time. The last thing he remembered was using his power to shock the unknown intruder in an attempt to stop him from entering the castle.

One of the workers held out a cup of water to Quinn. Quinn grasped the worker's arm and looked up at him in anguish. "What has that man done?" he cried.

Marlow, who had spent the last two years in the shape of a goat, was kneeling in bewilderment in a muddy castle pen amongst fourteen foul-smelling goats. Young Tobias, the castle goat herder, was shocked to see Marlow stumble out of his pen. Marlow looked up in confusion at the surprised boy and then back at the noisy goats. "I don't think I feel too good," he blubbered and collapsed into the boy's arms.

In fact, all of the people that had been transformed by Dryden instantly regained their natural forms with his defeat. Though they certainly remembered Dryden, they seemed to have little memory of their transformation and were shocked to hear what had happened to them and how things had changed throughout the land. Family members and friends rushed to welcome back and assist the dazed victims. Their reunions were happy and tearful.

Excitement was racing through the land, for word was quickly spreading that Dryden was defeated. The clouds had all but vanished, and the land was now basking in a brilliant sunshine that hadn't been seen in years. Word quickly spread throughout Acacia of the transmutant and the communicator. The people of Acacia flocked towards the castle.

Back at Glennon Village, workers were in a frenzy trying to clean up the fouled castle. Boards were being ripped from the windows and repairs were already underway. For the first time in a long time, laughter once again echoed throughout the castle. As villagers arrived, they quickly joined in to help clean and restore the castle. They laughed, sang, and joked as they worked; for once again, the castle belonged to them.

Afton helped her mother down to the castle library. They needed to get away from that awful room, and the library was close by at the bottom of the stairs. Scott followed Ogle down to the storage room to help Gregorian up to the library while Will looked for cloth to bandage a gash on Lewis's forehead.

The queen listened in shock as Afton explained to her all that had happened. She was overcome with heartache over the horrors that her people had suffered. She felt a gratitude without definition towards Scott, Will, and those who had helped to reclaim the castle.

The queen wiped a lone tear from her cheek. There would be much to do to restore Acacia to its former glory, and she knew it would have to begin with the healing process—first physically, then mentally and spiritually.

Ogle and Scott walked into the room with Gregorian limping between them. He used their shoulders to support the weight he couldn't put on his left leg. They led him over to a padded bench by a large stack of books.

Will staggered into the library behind them with Lewis lying limp in his arms, barely alive. He headed straight for the queen and set Lewis down on the table before her. Tears clouded his eyes. "Please help him," he begged. "He's my friend. He saved my life."

The queen placed her hand on Lewis's head and looked up at Will. "It is the very least I can do for you," she said, "for I owe you so much more."

With the touch of her hand, Lewis instantly jumped up to his feet and started waving his fists as if in the middle of a skirmish. "Where are those big, ugly, hairy things!" he yelled, scanning the room. "I ain't through with those buzzards yet!" As he searched the room, his eyes suddenly fell upon Will. With a leap of joy, he shot into Will's open arms. "Will! You're back!" he shrieked and hugged him hard. Will gave him a hard hug back, delighted to have his friend back as well.

Afton walked over to Gregorian, who was clapping and cheering along with the others as Will and Lewis embraced. "Mother, can you heal Gregorian's leg?" she asked. "He injured it defending me."

The queen smiled. "Certainly," she answered and walked over and placed her hand upon Gregorian's leg. "You have served your land well," she stated. "It will be duly noted in Acacian history."

Gregorian, overwhelmed with pride, rose to his feet—his leg completely healed—and bowed before the queen.

❧           ❧           ❧

After washing up and refreshing themselves, the queen led them all to a small, but elegantly furnished, room that led out to a balcony overlooking the castle's grand ballroom. Sounds of merriment and celebration echoed from every direction below. Food was brought in for them to eat, but they really hadn't found their appetites yet.

The room was beautiful, and it was one of the few spots in the castle that had been untouched by Dryden's wickedness. As they sat, Will filled the queen and the others in on the details of their final confrontation while Scott sat quietly and listened. He didn't want to talk about what had happened.

While the group sat in awe as Will finished telling them of the final moments, Ogle led Gwen, Brianna, and Dyana into the room. Gillean and Jonus, who were carrying Iris in on a makeshift stretcher, followed. Afton rushed to hug Gwen and was quickly joined by her mother. It was certainly a day in which tears ran freely—tears of joy and relief—as they all began to hug and commend each other in victory.

The queen went to Iris' side. "My daughter has told me of your bravery," she remarked as she placed her palm on Iris's injured leg. "Rise and be well."

Iris looked down at her leg where the beast had viciously bitten her. The wound had entirely disappeared. She climbed off of the stretcher and kneeled before the queen. "I again offer to you and the castle my services and loyalty."

The queen nodded and smiled. "And they will again be welcomed."

Ogle stepped forward and bowed. "Your Majesty, the Blackburn brothers have been secured in the storage cellar. What shall be done with them?"

The queen pondered the question for a moment. Never before did Acacia have to deal with any villainous behavior. Her decision would be a first. "It pains me to hear how they turned on their people," she replied and drew a deep breath. "For now, it is just important that I heal their minds of greed and their hearts of hate."

Scott was still sitting quietly on the bench next to Will and Lewis. He was glad everyone was happy again, but he just couldn't shake the brutal scene with Dryden from his mind. The queen noticed his inner struggle and walked over before him. "Please kneel before me," she requested and placed her hand on his forehead as he kneeled. "The land of Acacia owes you its thanks," she began. "Your time here will be one of legend. Let your heart and mind be healed of the terrible burden it carries. There was no other choice for you. Turning your back on Acacia would have been a far greater misdeed. Your heart is good and pure, young transmutant. You shall leave Acacia healthy of mind and spirit."

Scott felt as if a weight had been instantly lifted off of his shoulders and was struck with a realization that his experiences here were not to consume him but were to be learned from—to aid him in becoming a better person. Though it was horrible, the right thing had certainly been done.

The queen turned to the happy faces that filled the room. "Tonight, we will celebrate!"

And celebrate they did! Every member of Acacia had traveled to the castle. They filled the castle's grand ballroom and spilled out onto the large rear court to which it opened. Those with powers of music played songs that made people dance and sing and forget all of their troubles. The cooks busied themselves preparing roast and pheasant for all. Sweet juices flowed freely. The people hadn't felt happiness in a long time, and they were certainly making up for lost time.

The queen stepped out onto the large balcony that overlooked the ballroom. The crowd burst into cheer when they saw her. Their queen was back. With a wave of her hand, the crowd silenced in anticipation of her words.

"Today the land is ours once again!" the queen proclaimed and was answered by a resounding roar from the joyous people. Raising her hand, the people quieted as she continued: "We owe our thanks to several brave and courageous people, and I feel the need to recognize them." She then motioned for Gregorian and Chas to step forward. "Gregorian and Chas of the Bryce Village risked their lives to save our land. Their names will go down with distinction in Acacian history."

The crowd cheered wildly and called out to their heroes while Chas and Gregorian waved back to the spirited crowd.

The queen once more hushed the crowd and then signaled for her daughter Afton to step forward. "My daughter Afton has proven herself to be a capable leader during her quest to save Acacia. My heart overflows with pride." Afton curtsied to the cheering crowd and hugged her mother as the people cried out in adoration.

The queen next acknowledged the leaders from Bryce Village along with Iris for their vital roles in planning and supporting the recapture of the castle. Gillean, Dyana, Jonus, Brianna, Gwen, and Iris all bowed and waved.

The crowd now silenced in anticipation of the powerful outsiders who defeated Dryden and saved their land. The story of their final battle had spread, and everyone was eager to catch a glimpse of the communicator and transmutant.

The queen again stepped forward. "As many of you have already heard, we owe great thanks to two outsiders whose roles in reclaiming the land were of utmost importance; for these two outsiders faced and conquered Dryden."

The crowd erupted as the queen continued: "In the past we have felt uneasy about outsiders, and I think we've all learned a lesson from this. I know I have. These outsiders are good, and in the future we must be careful not to judge others unfairly."

She signaled for Will to stand next to her and turned towards the crowd. Lewis jumped up onto his shoulder. "People of Acacia, I give you Will, the communicator, and his faithful companion, Lewis."

The crowd went wild. Will wasn't quite sure what to do, so he bowed several times and waved back to the screaming Acacians. Lewis had both hands waving in the air and was blowing kisses. Will looked over at him and shook his head. "Will you knock that off!"

Lewis smiled down at him. "They love me!" he exclaimed and turned to blow an exaggerated kiss to the adoring crowd.

The queen next motioned for Scott to step forward. The people fell silent as he did. They looked up in awe at the powerful outsider who had ended Dryden's reign. The queen gently rested her hand on his shoulder. "People of Acacia," she announced, "I present to you Scott, the transmutant."

The crowd suddenly roared in unison. Their applause echoed throughout the castle and could be heard for miles around. Scott shuffled back and forth modestly and waved shyly. His wave brought another thunderous roar from the crowd. They cheered and cried out to the transmutant for several minutes before the queen silenced them. "From this moment on," she proclaimed, "I declare the communicator and the transmutant honorary citizens of Acacia. They will always have a home here at the castle." Approval roared throughout the people.

The queen then raised both of her hands above the crowd and shouted: "Let the celebration continue!" And with that, the musicians broke into song, and the people danced, sang, and lost themselves in merriment.

One of the traditional customs of celebration in Acacia is *The Display of Powers Dance*. In this, people join together in dance to form a large circle. People from the circle then individually step into the center of dancers and simply display their powers.

Afton grabbed Scott and Will and led them to the circle. They joined in and danced arm and arm. Lewis jumped on Will's shoulder and waved his hands back and forth in the air while swaying his hips from side to side in what he called the *Ferret Shuffle*.

A bright-eyed girl of about eleven from the Hadley Village named Elyza floated above the circle of dancers. They clapped and cheered in delight for the floating girl whose radiant smile infected the crowd. As she grew older, she would eventually become a *flyer*.

Before her, Dyana had pushed a tub of water into the circle and with a touch of her finger instantly turned the water to solid ice.

The ring of dancers started to chant for the transmutant, and it seemed as if the entire castle joined in. Will, who was dancing next to Scott, pushed him toward the middle. "C'mon. Show 'em what you've got!" he laughed.

As the dancers cheered him on, Scott reluctantly moved to the center and changed himself into the giant grizzly that had defeated the beasts. The circle momentarily fell back. Though they knew it was only Scott, the bear was still a horrible sight. Scott quickly turned himself back to normal, and the crowd roared. He next shifted to a huge elephant and then to a small mouse as the crowd cried out in astonishment and then clapped in delight. Returning to his natural form, Scott bowed and returned to his place in the circle next to Will.

Scott was a hard act to follow, but a man named Klar from the Alden Village, who has the power to double in size, was able to enchant the group.

Will clapped heartily before finally pulling Scott aside. "It's getting dark. We should start heading back," he pointed out. "When we entered Acacia, it was early afternoon back home but dusk had soon set in here. It must be early afternoon back at home, and Mom and Gramps will be expecting us back from camping soon. They'll start to worry if we stay out any longer."

Afton strolled over with two glasses filled with a cool brown liquid. "You two are dancing up a storm!" she laughed. "You must be thirsty." Will and Scott accepted the drinks but looked them over hesitantly. "It's just apple juice," Afton giggled. The boys blushed and gulped the juice down. It was sweet and delicious.

"I'll take a sip of that, too," squeaked Lewis, who was still puffing from his shuffle. The shuffle had actually caught on, and several Acacians were now doing it on the dance floor.

Will reached down and softly took Afton's hand in his. "We must be leaving soon," he said softly.

Afton's eyes welled up. She knew they would have to return sooner or later, but it still didn't make it any easier. "Will you come back?" she asked.

Will reached for her other hand and looked deeply into her eyes. "I promise," he whispered and gently kissed her on the forehead.

Afton led them to a small room off of the ballroom. Once there, Afton, Gregorian, Chas, Iris, the queen, and the other leaders from Bryce Village all gathered to say their final goodbyes to Scott and Will. They hugged and wept at their parting. After all they had experienced together, the bond between them would stay strong their entire lives.

Will hugged Chas strongly. "I have something for you," he whispered and unzipped a small compartment on the front of his backpack. Fumbling inside, he pulled out the Swiss Army knife that Gramps had given to him and Scott. Scott nodded in approval and smiled. "It'll come in handy next time you're exploring through the woods or something," said Will, and handed it to Chas.

Chas was astounded as he pulled out the different-sized blades, the scissors, the file, and the small magnifying glass. "What a magical tool!" he marveled.

Will just smiled. *They'd probably think our world is just as magical as their own,* he realized.

With final hugs and promises to return, Will and Scott slipped quietly out a side doorway. Once outside the castle wall, Scott changed himself back into the white stallion that Afton had rode in on. Will hopped onto its soft back with Lewis tucked comfortably away in the backpack. Lewis wasn't yet ready to say goodbye and had offered to guide them back to the pond that was his home.

Before leaving, they took one last look back at the castle and paused to listen to the celebration that roared on from inside. They both felt a true sense of satisfaction and a deep appreciation for the lessons the land had to offer.

Looking up, Will found Afton standing alone in a tower window. Will smiled and softly mouthed, "I'll return."

Afton smiled sadly and returned a soft, somber wave.

Will patted the mane of the fine beast and with an acknowledging whinny, the great white stallion turned and flashed off towards the pond that would bring them back home.

# CHAPTER 14

# Back at Grandpa's

The traveling back was much easier. Instead of sneaking through the dense undergrowth, they traveled the main road back to Bryce. Scott loped at a steady clip, and they were able to make the trip back to the village in little over two hours.

Scott slowed to a trot as Lewis guided him down the main road of the Village. Scott paused in front of Gwen's hut and let out a soft nicker. Will sighed from above and gently patted the velvety neck of the horse as Scott continued on toward the hill that led down to their gateway home.

As they approached the hilltop, they quietly looked down on the small, harmless pond. Will shook his head and exhaled loudly. "C'mon, little brother. Let's go home."

Scott carefully made the descent down to the bank and brought Will and Lewis to the large rock that they had first sat by with Afton the morning before. Will slid from the back of the white stallion and stretched while Scott changed to his normal form.

Lewis hopped out of Will's backpack and scurried onto the large rock. He struggled to keep control of his emotions; he would miss his friends. "Well, I guess this is it," he sniffed and stuck out his hand to shake exactly as he had done the day before when he had first met Will.

Will grabbed him with a hug. "I'll never forget what you did for me," he said. "You've been a truer friend than I've ever known."

Lewis couldn't hold back his tears any longer and finally let it all out, completely drenching Will's shoulder. "Just promise you'll come back and visit someday, okay?" he sobbed.

"You can bet on it," Will promised.

Scott walked over and hugged Lewis also. Lewis started once again with a fresh set of tears that soaked Scott's shirt as well. "I'll never forget you," said Scott. "And don't worry, Lewis; we'll see you again."

Scott and Will took one last look around the pond. What they had experienced here in the last twenty-four hours or so was simply unbelievable. Will let out a long, deep breath and tousled Scott's hair. Scott shook his head in wonder.

As Lewis watched from the top of the rock, the boys splashed back into the pond and trudged towards its center. They paused to give a final look back to their furry, little friend, who was still sobbing as he slumped on top of the boulder. Lewis flashed a thumbs-up sign. Smiling, Scott and Will waved a final good-bye before plunging beneath the water's surface and out of Acacia.

❦         ❦         ❦

As Scott and Will scanned the bottom of the pond, they spotted the entrance to their bedroom through some algae near the back bank of the pond. It looked almost as if there were a large oval window lying against the pond's edge and through it they could clearly see into the bedroom. It appeared empty.

Will stuck his head through the orb and peered into the bedroom. Water dripped from his head and splattered loudly on the wooden floor. Scott stuck his head through just below Will and took in a deep breath of air. Will signaled to keep quiet, so they could hear if Mother or Gramps were home. He glanced over at the alarm clock on top of the bureau. It read 3:11. He strained to listen for any signs of his mother or grandfather, but the house was silent. "They must be out somewhere," he whispered. "Let's go."

Will pulled himself through the orb and grabbed hold of Scott's arm to help him through. "Now let's get rid of these things," he said, pulling the amulet from his neck.

"Bye, orb," said Scott, and with a quick motion, pulled the amulet over his head and handed it to Will. Will carefully placed them back into the box and secured them in the drawer's secret compartment.

Scott peered down at the water that had spilled onto the bedroom floor. "We'd better get some towels," he suggested and dashed into the bathroom to retrieve some from the closet. He threw one to Will, and the boys worked quickly to dry up the floor before changing out of their wet clothes.

"Where's the camping stuff?" asked Will, as he pulled a clean shirt over his head.

Scott finished tying up his sneaker. "It's right here," he replied, reaching under the bed.

"We might as well bring it downstairs and put it away," said Will.

It took two trips, but the boys managed to return the tent under the cellar stairs and put the sleeping bags back into their grandfather's storage closet. The only thing left to do was to return the fishing poles to the shed and then find Mom and Gramps.

Will grabbed the tackle box while Scott grabbed the two poles, and they headed out back. "I kinda miss Acacia already," sighed Will.

"Me, too," replied Scott. "I was just trying to see if I could change into something, but nothing happened."

As Scott opened the shed door, Mother and Gramps stepped into the backyard from a path that led to the lake. "There you two are," said Mother. "We looked everywhere for you. We were getting worried."

"Thank the Good Spirits," whispered Gramps.

"We just got back," replied Will.

"Where did you camp?" asked Gramps. "We looked up by the old site, but we couldn't find any trace of yeh."

"We…ah…tried a new place on the other end of the lake," answered Scott.

"We almost thought the tiger got yeh," growled Gramps.

"No, he didn't get us," smirked Will.

Scott tried not to laugh.

"Well, did you catch Ol' Bess?" asked Mom.

"No luck," answered Scott.

"Maybe we'll try for her tomorrow if the rain holds off," said Gramps. "You don't know how worried you boys had me."

"No need to worry, Gramps. We can take care of ourselves," said Scott.

"That I know. That I know," replied Gramps, tousling Scott's hair. "C'mon. You must be starvin'. I've got some left-over chili in the freezer. All it needs is a little hot sauce."

Following their grandfather through the kitchen door, Scott and Will plopped down at the large oak table. They were exhausted. "You two will sleep good tonight," noticed Gramps. "You boys take it easy now. I'll get supper ready and then start a fire."

Will rested his elbows on the table and sank his head into his hands. He happened to notice a little bug scurrying across the kitchen floor, a beetle. Will watched curiously as it tried to make its way under the cabinets. He shook his head and sighed with relief, but just then, Gramps raised a foot to step on the little critter.

"Don't!" yelled Will.

Gramps stumbled back in surprise. "It's only a bug."

"I'm sorry," Will apologized. "I didn't mean to yell. I just kinda like beetles," he explained and scooped the little beetle onto a piece of paper as Gramps looked on in astonishment. "I know how you feel, little guy," Will whispered and let it free out back.

Will returned to the table and sat down next to his mother. Scott leaned over and chuckled. Will grinned and winked back at him.

Mother could only shake her head as she put her arms around the boys. "I hope you boys are having a good time," she said.

"It's been unbelievable," smiled Will.

"More than unbelievable," added Scott.

Mother returned their smiles. "I'm glad. I was afraid you boys might get a little bored this year."

Gramps smiled and shook his head. Scott and Will just looked at each other and burst into laughter.

# Author's Note

I completed the first draft of *Amulets of Acacia* back in May of 1994. The manuscript was initially titled *Into the Mirror*, and instead of having amulets create an orb, I used a mirror as the magical gateway into the land of what was then called *Betania*. It was my first attempt at writing a children's novel, and the fact that I even completed it was a triumph in itself. My triumph, though, was dulled somewhat as I stepped back to realistically assess the manuscript. The story simply lacked novelty—a blend of sorts of one of my favorite children's books, C. S. Lewis's *The Lion, the Witch and the Wardrobe*, with a childhood passion of mine, Marvel Comics.

After a few half-hearted attempts at getting the manuscript published, I shelved the idea and decided to use the manuscript as a tool in my elementary classroom. Students lined up to read the manuscript, and the discussions it created not only helped shape my writing style but inspired writing in students as well. I realized how important it was that students viewed me as a writer first and not just somebody who talked about writing.

I loved to tell of the day in which I wrote my favorite chapter, *Attack of the Beasts*. It was a day in which I was lost in *the zone* as I like to call it. I acted out each scene in my living room (I would have looked a crazy man if anyone had happened by) and then tried to transform those actions and emotions onto paper. Morning slipped into afternoon—late night...Thereafter, I would see students in class acting out situations as they wrote, and a smile would cross my face. Students marveled when I told them I would sometimes spend hours—even days—on one sentence or paragraph to capture a certain flow or feeling.

As years passed, something more important finally dawned on me: Children simply loved the manuscript. And isn't that what writing is truly about? Maybe, to me, the story lacked novelty, but to the children it contained an ingredient even more important: *magic.* Students loved to share the powers they dreamed of having if they could enter Acacia. They debated powers and discussed favorite characters and scenes—they laughed, they dreamed, they cared, they were inspired...It was time to publish the manuscript—for them.

The changing of the mirror to an amulet has created much debate amongst readers. Some prefer the more mature, sci-fi element of the orb, whereas others prefer the simplistic nature of the mirror. The solution? One that I believe may be a first: an alternate beginning. Read on and decide for yourself—but more importantly, laugh, dream, care, be inspired...enjoy!

# Alternate Beginning
## Into the Mirror

# *Prologue*

The old man couldn't seem to shake the weird feeling that had come over him. It was the mirror. The feeling had hit him the moment he'd laid eyes on it.

"C'mon, old man," he mumbled to himself as he leaned on a nearby table to catch his breath, "stop being silly."

The old man took a deep breath and steadied himself. He had been excited about this auction for weeks now and wasn't about to let an old mirror spook him, not with all the good stuff to be had here today.

With a brisk shake of his head, the old man hobbled over towards a row of mismatched furniture—anything to get away from the odd mirror—but the strange feeling followed. He wouldn't say it was a bad feeling—or a good feeling for that matter. It was just a feeling that something strange was happening that he didn't quite understand yet. He tried to just ignore it and turn his attention to a crate of old tools, but no matter how hard he tried to look them over, his eyes kept wandering back to the mirror. The feeling was overpowering.

Deciding a little fresh air might help, the old man started for the door but suddenly spun back in disbelief. He had heard a voice—a voice that was different from those murmuring about the room. It was soft, yet troubled—a young girl's;

he was almost certain, but it had a different echo to it as if it had sounded from a distant place that was not of the room. Though no one else browsing about the room's items seemed to take notice, he could have sworn it had come from the mirror.

Swallowing hard, the old man stumbled back towards the odd piece. He stood before it for what seemed like many minutes just staring back at his reflection and listening, but there was nothing more to be heard.

"Your age is finally catchin' up to you, old man," he muttered wearily.

He did have to admit, though, there was definitely something strange about the mirror, but what seemed even stranger still was that he wanted it—or was it that the mirror wanted him? He was struck with a certainty that in some mysterious way it was meant to be his; that this was what the strange feeling was all about though he wasn't quite sure why. He didn't need a mirror, and as far as mirrors went, it was rather bizarre looking, but he was sure as fate that there was a place for it somewhere in his house, a place where it was meant to stand.

*The boys' room*, he smiled. That's where he'd put it, the room where his grandsons stayed when they came to visit. *They'd probably get a kick out of the old thing*, he grinned. In fact, he was sure they would.

# CHAPTER 1

# *On to Grandpa's*

"Entering Massachusetts!" blurted Scott.

Mother just smiled. Scott didn't get quite as excited as he used to when the faded-blue sign came into view, but he still yelled it out anyway. He had taken over the role several years before by beating Mother to the punch one trip and had assumed the duty ever since. It was a matter of tradition now.

On one trip when Scott was about six, Mother had actually pulled the car over so she and Scott could jump back and forth across the state line. Scott had told everyone that summer how he'd jumped from Rhode Island to Massachusetts. It was one of his favorite memories. He still thought about it every time they passed the old sign.

"We'll be there before you know it," said Mother, watching Scott in the rearview mirror.

Scott just leaned his head back against the window. They had been driving now for almost five hours, and he was fresh out of ways to entertain himself. The bag of chips had emptied a good hour before, and his eyes were too tired for him to read any more from the book he was reading about the Civil

War called *Fife*. He had had enough reading for one day, anyway.

Will, his older brother, was slumped in the front seat with his headphones on and was staring straight ahead with a completely blank expression. This was the first year that Will gave Mother a hard time about going to Grandpa's—something about missing out on everything. He had barely spoken a word since they left. His headphones were blaring so loudly that Scott could make out the songs from the back seat.

They had been making this ride at the beginning of every summer for as long as Scott could remember. Mother felt it was important for the boys to spend time with their grandfather, so just after school closing each year, they would pack their bags and head north to spend a week at Grandpa's. For Scott and Will it came to mark the beginning of summer vacation.

Gramps lived in a small ranch-style house near a lake that was surrounded by towering pines. Will once heard him say he owned more than fourteen acres of land, and it was chock-full of places to explore and things to do. Their old tree fort would certainly be in need of repair, and Ol' Bess was still out there for the challenge—a two-foot bass that was as sly as a fox. Scott came close to pulling her in last year, but the crafty old fish snapped the line before Gramps could get a net on her—maybe this year.

The trip was special for Mother too. For her it meant relaxation. She would say the trip was spiritual—a week to take it easy and leave all the pressures of life behind. She and Gramps would search out yard sales and take long walks through the woods and talk about nothing and everything. Gramps pampered her the entire stay, and Mother gladly let him. Gramps knew how hard she worked all year to take care of the boys and felt it was the least she deserved.

Mother was a gentle woman and the glue that held the family together, especially after Scott and Will's father passed away several years before. It was a difficult time for all of them, but she somehow found the strength to pull them all through it. Their trips to Grandpa's took on even more importance then.

Scott was a surprisingly tall, but thin, ten-year-old with straight brown hair and deep blue eyes. Though an average student, he had a kind heart and was well liked at school. He was a pretty good athlete too. Hockey and baseball were his favorites, and he was good at both.

Will had just turned fifteen and was experimenting with growing his hair long. He had curly hair, and Scott thought it was just getting puffier, but Will thought it made him look older. He had been taking guitar lessons for the past year and was hoping to start a band soon with some of the guys from school.

Will was at the age where it wasn't cool to be hanging out with family, so he decided to just tune them out instead. Mother refused to let it dampen her spirits though. She was too excited about seeing her father again to let it.

"Just ten more minutes," she announced, noticing Scott's boredom (That seemed to be one of her favorite lines.).

"That's what you said ten minutes ago," moaned Scott.

"Well, we're almost there. The old clock tower's right up ahead."

The first sight of the old clock tower always welled up a good feeling inside of Scott's chest. The tower was atop an old church and had read 6:33 for the past fourteen years. It had become a well-known landmark in the area. Even Will took off his headphones at the sight of it.

"I think I can smell Grandpa's chili already," chuckled Mother.

Every summer it was the same thing. They would pull up, and Gramps would run out and yell, "Hurry up! The chili's ready, and it's burning a hole through the pot!"

It was good chili, but the taste seemed to linger for days. Gramps loved it hot. In fact, he loved everything hot. He even put Tabasco sauce on his eggs in the morning much to the boys' disgust.

"Are you going to try to catch Ol' Bess this year?" Mother asked Will in an attempt to arouse some excitement in him.

It looked as if Will was starting to come around. The sight of the old clock tower couldn't help but bring back good memories and feelings, but he stubbornly continued to brood. "Maybe," he muttered.

"Hey, Will. Do you think the fort's still up?" asked Scott, as he tugged at Will's shoulder.

Will tried to just shrug him off but finally caved in and smiled for the first time since they left. Though he'd never admit it, he was curious himself to see how the old fort had survived. "We can check it out tomorrow, if you want," he offered and reached back to tousle Scott's hair.

As they rounded the last bend by *Mama Pedroli's Pizza & Pastrami*, they started down the long dirt road that would lead them to their grandfather's. A kind of hushed excitement came over them as it did every year when they turned down the old dirt way. The road was always dry, and as usual, the dust engulfed the car, temporarily blinding them, but as the car slowed, the dust began to settle, and Grandpa's house slowly came into view.

The old place never seemed to change, thought Scott. The faded shingles may have been a bit more faded, but the same dented red mailbox hung unevenly by the door, the same assortment of worn wicker chairs littered the porch, and the same old gray statue of a lion sat stoically by the bottom stair (Gramps had spotted it at some old yard sale.). "He guards the property," Gramps would say of the stone beast.

As the car sputtered to a halt, Mother gave a couple of "toots" on the horn. As if on cue, Gramps came bounding out the front door. "Hurry up!" he puffed.

"We know," smiled Will, as he opened the car door. "The chili's ready, and it's burning a hole in the pot."

"Dang tootin'!" cried Gramps. "Just leave them bags in the car. We'll get 'em later. Now get over here and give me a hug before my house burns down!"

Gramps was a surprisingly robust man for his age. He had arms like a bear and gave the kind of hugs that swallowed you whole. Though they always kept in touch throughout the year, it felt good to see him again.

A large stone fireplace dominated the inside of the house, and in the kitchen stood the longest oak table the boys had ever seen. Gramps loved to go hunting for antiques, and there wasn't a yard sale for miles around that he didn't sniff out. He furnished his house this way. It was full of odd and different kinds of furnishings, mostly old and what might seem like junk to others, but a *find* for Gramps. All that stuff, though, seemed to find its proper place and provided the house with a warm, homey feeling.

Four bowls of piping-hot chili were already sitting on the kitchen table when they stepped in. They sat right away, and Gramps took a loaf of warm bread out of the oven. The sweet aroma filled the room, reminding them all of how hungry they were. Gramps sliced them each a large piece and smothered them in butter. They plunged into the chili. Though it always took a couple of bites and a few gulps of water before they got used to the spice, they were hungry, and that made it seem even more delicious.

"Boy, you two have gotten big!" exclaimed Gramps. "Your mom must be feedin' you pretty good back home."

"They eat me out of house and home!" giggled Mother.

"Did I tell you boys I almost caught Ol' Bess?" said Gramps. "I had her on the line for almost half a minute before she broke free. I'm countin' on you two boys to finally get her this year."

"We'll have her in the pan by the week's end," vowed Will.

Gramps snorted in approval and rumpled Will's hair. "Now finish up that chili, everyone!" he bellowed. "I've got an apple pie warming in the oven and a full pint of cookie-dough ice cream in the freezer."

"Awesome!" cried Scott.

"How about you, Mums?" Gramps asked. "Pie and ice cream?"

"Only if you promise to walk it off with me tomorrow," she replied.

"Deal," Gramps agreed.

After dinner the boys got their bags from the car and dragged them into the room that they would share for the next week. The room hadn't changed much over the years. It consisted of a big wooden bunk bed and matching bureaus. A painting of a mare and her foal hung over one of the bureaus, and an old floor lamp stood next the other (Gramps had surely found them at some old yard sale.). In the far corner of the room next to the bureaus was a door that led to an adjacent bathroom and directly across from that, a closet. The trains that dotted the wallpaper seemed cool when they were younger but were a bit annoying now.

The only new addition to the room was an odd-looking mirror that loomed in the corner like an ancient warrior of some type. It was oval in shape and unusually big. It sat within a heavy wooden stand and looked to Will and Scott as if it might have been the oldest thing they'd ever seen. On the mirror's thick wooden frame were carvings that appeared to be symbols of some sort. They reminded Will of the types he'd seen when his class had studied Ancient Egypt—*Hyrogriffics*, as Scott used to call them, but not quite the same. It was a peculiar piece of furniture for sure.

"That mirror's creepy," Scott frowned.

"It certainly is weird looking," Will agreed. "I wonder where Gramps picked it up."

Just then, Mother poked her head into the room. Both boys jumped. "I'm sorry. I didn't mean to startle you," she chuckled. "Your grandfather is starting a fire. We can play some cards before you head to bed, if you want."

"Sounds good," said Will. "Tell Gramps he's goin' down this year."

*Rummy 500* was the game, and Gramps was the champ. He would always hold on to all of his *straights* and *threes-of-a-kind* and wait for that one card he needed to go out and leave everyone stranded with all of their cards. Will came close to beating him once last year, but Gramps stuck him with two *aces* in the final hand to win the game.

"C'mon," said Will. "We can finish unpacking tomorrow. You're going down, too."

Scott just rolled his eyes. He always got creamed when they played cards, and he really wasn't in the mood for another humiliating defeat. Will rushed out to the den, though, leaving Scott with little choice. Before following, Scott paused in front of the mirror and swept a hand through his hair. A weird feeling suddenly struck him. At first he thought it might have been the chili, but he couldn't seem to shake it. It wasn't a bad feeling, but he wouldn't say it was a good one, either. It was just a feeling that something was about to happen—*something big.*

## CHAPTER 2

# *The Mirror*

Scott hadn't realized how tired he was until he settled down at the table to play cards. The drive had really knocked him out, and he found himself dozing off as the game wore on. He was losing bigtime, anyway. Gramps was way ahead as usual and kept whistling some annoying tune from about fifty years ago. Will was really irritated.

Mother was hanging in there, but it didn't really matter to her whether she won or lost—it never did. She just loved the fact that everyone was together. "Why don't you head to bed," she whispered to Scott. "You'll need your rest if you're going to rebuild the fort tomorrow."

Scott nodded wearily and forced himself up with a yawn. "You win, Gramps," he conceded.

Gramps sprung from his chair and tousled Scott's hair (He was always doing that.). "You played me hard this year, *Tiger.* C'mon. I'll walk you down to the room."

"Make sure you come back," barked Will. "This ain't over yet."

Will never did take losing very well. Gramps was up by over a hundred points and was holding on to his cards again. That meant trouble for Will.

Scott smirked as he entered the bedroom. "Looks like I get the top bunk again."

Gramps stooped to click on a metal fan that was resting on the near bureau. "First come—first served. You sleep tight now, you hear?"

"Thanks, Gramps," smiled Scott. It certainly did feel good to see Gramps again.

Gramps leaned over, kissed Scott on the forehead, and tousled his hair. "Now to finish off that grumpy ol' brother of yours," he snorted, and with a quick wink, gently closed the door behind him.

Scott threw on a T-shirt and the worn flannel shorts that he usually wore to bed and went into the bathroom to wash-up. When he finished, he climbed onto the top bunk, clicked off the light, and settled under the covers. He enjoyed the minutes lying in bed before sleep overtook him; it was when he did his best thinking. Tonight, though, he was exhausted and fading quickly.

As Scott's thoughts swirled into dream, a strange noise jolted him awake. It had sounded like someone was crying. He strained to listen further, but the room settled back into silence. Probably just Will losing, he figured, and with a gaping yawn, rolled back onto his side.

As his thoughts drifted away once more, the strange sound again filled the room. Somebody was definitely crying, and it wasn't Will. It sounded like a young girl, and it was coming from the closet.

In one frantic move Scott leaned over the side of the bunk and flipped on the light. Tumbling out of the bunk, he lurched towards the door. As he reached for the door's knob, another soft whimper echoed from the closet—but instead of getting out of there, Scott found himself moving towards the closet door. It was as if a huge human magnet of sorts were pulling him towards it.

He paused in front of the closet and slowly reached for the closet's handle. It felt cold on his skin. His hand shook. With a deep breath he pushed down the handle and slowly pulled open the door. He was ready to make a run for it, if he had to, but when he peeked in, there was nothing there but some old flannel shirts.

Gramps should definitely check this out, he decided, and retreated towards the bedroom door. But just as he reached it, the weeping that continued from behind halted him once again. He had been wrong. It wasn't coming from the closet. It seemed to be coming from behind the strange mirror that stood next to it. Could a small girl be crouched behind it? Scott slowly leaned to the side to peek behind the mirror, but there was nothing behind it that he could see. Oddly, though, the sobbing continued.

Inching closer, Scott paused before the tall mirror and examined it more closely. The crying wasn't coming from behind it, he realized, but seemed to be coming from it. A crying mirror?

Reaching out a finger, Scott lightly touched the mirror and gasped. He couldn't believe what was happening. It felt as if he were touching the surface of water. Ripples extended out from the point at which his finger touched what was supposed to be solid glass. He was even more astonished to find that the tip of his finger was actually wet.

Scott stared dumbfounded as the ripples settled upon the mirror. He hesitated but again reached out to touch the smooth surface. This time his finger actually penetrated the mirror's face. It felt as if he were dipping his hand into a fish tank. It was definitely water; it dripped down his fingers and onto the floor, but why wasn't it pouring out into the room?

Scott listened in bewilderment to the weeping that seemed to be coming from just beyond the water's surface. He tried to see if he could peer in, but only his reflection stared back at him. He inched in closer still and even tried to peer in from different angles, but he still couldn't make out anything beyond his own image.

Finally, he crept in so close that his nose actually brushed the mirror's surface so that he could feel the cool wetness upon it. Instead of pulling back, though, he continued to press in further and actually found himself taking a deep breath. To his own surprise he suddenly plunged his entire head into the mirror.

His head was under water, or should I say—*in water*! He looked up in utter astonishment. He could see rays of sunlight shimmering through what appeared to be the surface of a shallow pond that his head was now thrust into. Wherever it was, it appeared as if a morning sun was in the midst of rising. He judged the surface to be about four feet up and could make out the outline of trees and clouds in the sky above. Kneeling by the bank was a girl.

Scott jerked his head out of the mirror and gasped for air. His head was drenched, and he was dripping all over the bedroom floor. He quickly checked behind the mirror again, but there was nothing there but floor and wall. *Was he dreaming?* He couldn't be. He was soaked!

Scott rushed into the bathroom to get a towel and stopped short in front of the mirror above the sink. He gave it a quick poke and exhaled in relief—it was solid.

As Scott changed his T-shirt, Will strolled into the bedroom. "Gramps won again," he moaned and then noticed the puddles of water leading into the bathroom. "Hey! Why is the floor all wet? You didn't—"

"No!" exclaimed Scott. "Will, I know you're not going to believe me, but it's that mirror. You've got to go over and touch it."

Will looked confused. "Why? What's going on?"

"Please, Will. Go over and touch the mirror," Scott pleaded.

With a look of utter confusion and concern on his face, Will glanced at the mirror and back at Scott before slowly starting towards it. He knelt down before the mirror and inspected it closely. "What's wrong with it?"

"Go ahead," Scott urged. "Touch it."

Will cautiously raised a finger. As he touched it, ripples again raced across its surface. "What the heck?" he gasped. "What's going on, Scott?"

Scott was glad that Will also saw that this was no regular mirror. He almost thought for a moment that he might be going crazy. "Do you hear it?" Scott asked.

"Yeah," Will answered. He looked as if he were hearing a ghost. "Is that somebody crying?"

"It's a girl crying," explained Scott. "I stuck my head into the mirror to see who it was. That's why I'm wet. It's some kind of pond, Will, and the girl crying is sitting by the bank of it."

"We should get Gramps," said Will. "Maybe he knows about this."

Scott looked down at the wet floor. "We should clean this up first before he comes in, just in case."

Scott grabbed two towels from the bathroom and threw one to Will. Together they wiped up the wet floor as best they could before calling in Gramps.

"Is everything all right?" answered Mom, from down the hall.

"Yeah, fine, Mom," Scott replied. "We just need to ask Gramps something."

"I'm on my way, *Tiger*," puffed Gramps, as he lumbered down to the bedroom. "What's up, boys?" he asked, poking his head into the room.

"Gramps, where did you get that mirror?" Will asked.

"Strange piece, isn't it?" Gramps replied. "I got that mirror at an auction a few towns over. It belonged to a man that had disappeared two years back or so—a strange case. It still baffles the police," explained Gramps. "The bank took over his house and auctioned it off along with all of the furniture in it. That mirror just caught my eye. There's just something about it I can't seem to place my finger on. I knew you boys would get a kick out of it."

As Gramps explained the story to them, he walked over, pulled a rag out from his back pocket, and leaned over to dust off the mirror. Scott and Will held their breath, but when Gramps started to wipe clean the surface of the mirror, there were no ripples! Why wasn't his hand going through the surface as Scott and Will's had? Gramps continued to clean off the glass and then stepped back to admire his efforts. "There," he said. "There's just something about this mirror."

Scott looked at Will and shrugged his shoulders.

"Anything else I can help you boys with?" asked Gramps.

"No," answered Will, in a daze. "Thanks."

They didn't dare say anything about the water and the girl crying now that nothing happened when Gramps touched the mirror. He'd think they were crazy or something.

Gramps said good night and left the boys staring dumbly at each other and wondering whether they just might be going crazy or not. Will walked over to the mirror and touched it. To his surprise he felt the solid surface of glass—no ripples or water. "It's back to normal," he pointed out.

"I don't hear the crying anymore, either," Scott remarked. "What happened, Will?"

"I don't know, Scott. Maybe Grandpa's chili finally got to us."

Neither of them really believed this, but they left it at that for now. Scott climbed back into the top bunk while Will washed up. He knew it really happened; his hair was still damp. As Will came in from the bathroom, his bare foot slid on a spatter of water they had missed. It was all he could do to just keep his balance before crawling into the bottom bunk.

"Will?"

"Yeah?"

"Do you mind if we keep the light on for a while?" asked Scott.

"No, that's okay," Will answered. He really didn't mind having the light on for a while himself.

"Do you think she'll come back, Will…the girl crying?"

"I don't know, Scott…I really don't know."

Both boys lay in their beds quietly for what seemed like hours, just staring at the mirror before sleep finally overtook them both.

## CHAPTER 3

# *The Girl by the Bank*

Both boys found themselves that night in dreams that swirled around the mirror. Will dreamed of plunging deep into the mirror's water, far from the surface. He thrashed and rolled in his bed as he desperately tried to reach air in his dream. Panic overwhelmed him until his dream suddenly transformed with the soft melody of a ballad that was so sweet and pure that he found himself floating peacefully upwards as the heavenly song guided him to the surface and fresh air.

Scott dreamed of a hand that shot through the mirror and grabbed him by the arm. The grip was strong. He couldn't pull away. It was dragging him into the mirror. His body jerked in bed as he struggled with the powerful hand of his dream. Suddenly, he too heard a song—a wonderful and beautiful song. It had an instant calming effect. The hand abruptly let go and disappeared back into the mirror as Scott slipped into a peaceful dream in which he found himself floating on water in a state of total tranquility.

Scott slowly awoke from his dream. The window's shade wasn't drawn completely allowing for the morning sunlight to pour in. His eyes struggled with the fresh light as his surroundings came into focus, but was he still hearing the singing?

Scott shot up in bed and quickly scanned the room. The sweet song that floated through his dreams was still being sung, and it was coming from the mirror.

Scott swung his head over the edge of the bunk and reached down to tug Will's shoulder. "Will, wake up!" he whispered. "Wake up!"

Will roused with a start. "What?" he grunted and then instantly realized that he, too, was still hearing the tender ballad that had come to his rescue in his dream. "I heard that singing in my dream last night," he whispered.

"Me, too. It's coming from the mirror."

The singing abruptly stopped. The boys stared anxiously at the mirror waiting for the melody to continue—something—but only the sounds of a waking house filled the air.

Mother poked her head into the room. "Are you boys going to sleep all morning? I need your help out in the kitchen. I'm making pancakes, and your grandfather's trying to put hot sauce in the batter. Quick!"

Will put on a smile. "We'll be right out."

"Should we tell them?" whispered Scott.

Will hesitated. "It seems to keep stopping whenever they come in," he pointed out. "They're never going to believe us, and Mom will just start worrying. Let's just wait and see if anything else happens."

The boys quickly threw on their jeans and sneakers and started for the kitchen but before leaving, took a last, uneasy glance back at the mirror.

"Get away from those pancakes, Gramps!" yelled Will, as he entered the kitchen. "My tongue is still trying to recover from your chili last night!"

"A little spice never hurt no pancakes," snickered Gramps.

"You're gross, Gramps!" snorted Scott.

Mother made good pancakes—big and fluffy—and Gramps made the syrup himself from a maple tree out back. It was sweet, thick, and delicious.

The batter was saved from Grandpa's hot sauce, but his pancakes weren't so lucky. He smothered each cake not only with syrup, but with Tabasco sauce as well.

"That's disgusting!" moaned Scott.

"Have you ever tried it?" asked Gramps.

Scott just stuck his tongue out in disgust.

Mother laughed. "Your grandfather and I are going hunting for yard sales today. Do you boys want to come with us?"

Will had the syrup bottle turned completely upside down and was drowning his pancakes in syrup. "Nah, I think I'm gonna see if the old tree fort is still up," he replied.

"Me, too," added Scott.

"That sounds fun," Mother smiled. "Just make sure you boys stay together, okay?"

"We will," mumbled Will, through a mouthful of pancake. Will always ate like it was his last meal.

After breakfast Mother and Gramps got ready to leave for their day of rummaging while Scott and Will put on clean shirts and made plans to head out to the fort.

Mom kissed them both before she left. "Be careful," she warned.

"Watch out for mountain lions," teased Gramps.

"There's no mountain lions out there, Gramps!" exclaimed Will.

"There's bears, though," he said with a growl.

Mother gave Gramps a playful slap on the arm. "Stop that, Dad! You'll scare Scott."

"I'm not scared!" shot Scott. "I know there's no bears out there!"

"Well, make sure you stay clear of the snakes, then," hissed Gramps. "There's some nasty ones out there."

"That's enough," giggled Mother. "Let's go before the boys decide to stay in."

Gramps laughed and carefully placed his lucky exploring hat—as he called it—on his head, nothing but a limp, brown-leather cowboy hat of sorts. Gramps never left the house without it and had been wearing it for as long as Scott and Will could remember. Mom used to try to talk him into getting a new hat, but Gramps refused to part with his lucky exploring hat.

As Mother closed the door behind them, the boys quickly set about gathering supplies. Scott headed down into the basement to find a hammer and some nails while Will headed out back to sort through a pile of discarded wood behind the shed. Most of the wood had rotted out, but some of the boards underneath had been sheltered from the weather and were still in good shape. Will set aside a few of the sturdier boards and headed back into the house to help Scott.

Scott was at work in the kitchen filling up an old backpack with junk food and sodas. "I found some good boards out back," said Will, as he entered through the back door. "Did you find the hammer?"

Scott didn't answer, though—couldn't answer. He was frozen stiff. The bag of chips dropped from his hand and splattered about the kitchen floor. Will whirled in alarm. The faint sobs of a young girl were echoing from the bedroom.

Scott started to panic. "Let's get out of here and find Mom and Gramps, Will."

"They're long gone," said Will. "We'll never find them."

Scott was frightened. The crying was getting louder. "Then what are we going to do?" he cried.

Will shot a glance down towards the bedroom. "C'mon. Let's find out what's going on."

The two boys inched their way down towards the bedroom and paused at the foot of the door. They stood there for quite some time, just listening, as the cries of the weeping girl sounded from the room. Neither wanted to step in first.

"Go ahead," urged Scott.

Will figured he was the oldest and summoned up some courage. "Okay. Follow me," he said, and with a deep breath cautiously stepped into the room. Scott latched onto the back of his shirt and followed.

Will crept over to the mirror and leaned before it. He slowly reached out to touch its surface. Ripples raced to the frame at the touch of his finger. He glanced back at Scott, who was standing wide-eyed behind him and then back at the mirror. A determined look swept over Will's face, and with a quick breath he grabbed a firm hold of the mirror's frame and plunged his head through the surface.

Will couldn't believe what was happening. His head was definitely submerged in a pond or lake of some kind. Peering down, he could see the algae and rocks of the bottom and as he looked up, the sky and the outline of trees through the surface—and there, kneeling by the bank, he could make out the outline of a girl.

Will pulled his head from the mirror and gasped for air. "I saw her! It's unbelievable!" he cried.

"Let's get out of here," urged Scott.

"I'm going in," Will announced.

"What!" cried Scott. "What if you can't get back?"

"Just hold on to my hand while I go in. You can pull me back if I need you to."

But Scott wasn't so sure. "Don't," he begged.

Will was determined, though. "It'll be okay. Just keep hold of my arm."

Will grabbed the top of the mirror with one hand and slowly pushed his head and shoulder into the mirror. Scott grabbed a firm hold of Will's arm and held on tightly as Will continued to force his body through the mirror.

The cool water swallowed Will up as he pushed farther in. With a final thrust he drove his entire body through the mirror and into the pond of the strange new world. Scott held on for dear life from the other side.

Will stuck his head back through the mirror and into the bedroom. The sight of just his head sticking out from the mirror was an eerie sight. Scott stumbled back. Water dripped from Will's head onto the floor as he regained his breath. "It's okay," he said. "It's so weird. I can see right into the bedroom from in here. I'm going up. Come with me."

"I don't want to, Will," pleaded Scott.

Will reached his hand out through the mirror. "It's okay. Take my hand," he urged.

Scott realized Will wasn't going to give him much of a choice and reluctantly took his hand. With a fainthearted gulp Scott forced his way into the mirror as Will pulled from the other side.

0-595-27163-4

Printed in the United States
27138LVS00002B/61